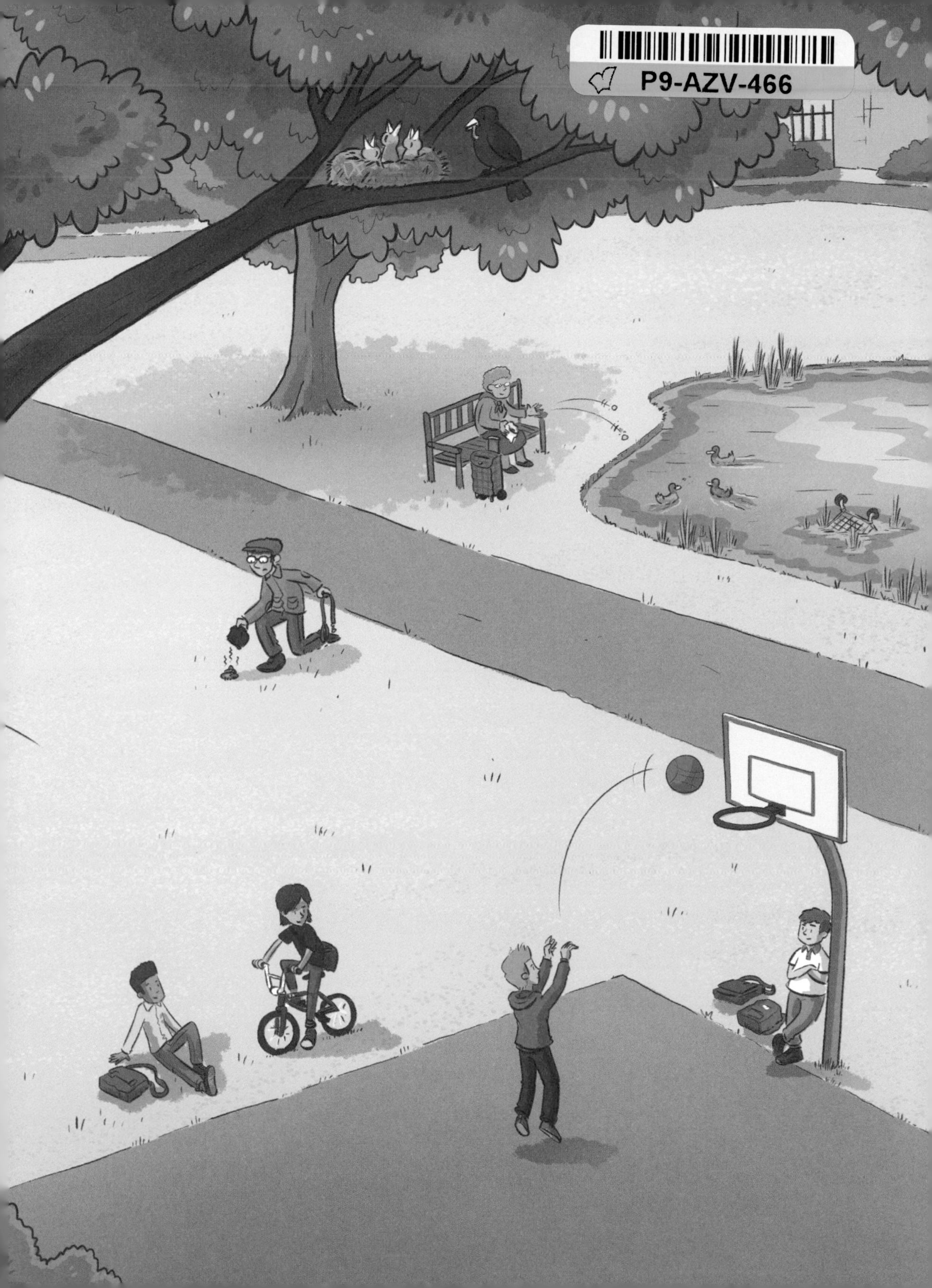

First published in 2018
by Singing Dragon
an imprint of Jessica Kingsley Publishers
73 Collier Street
London N1 9BE, UK
and
400 Market Street, Suite 400
Philadelphia, PA 19106, USA

www.singingdragon.com

Library of Congress Cataloging in Publication Data
A CIP catalog record for this book is available from the Library of Congress

British Library Cataloguing in Publication Data
A CIP catalogue record for this book is available from the British Library

ISBN 978 1 84819 330 7
eISBN 978 0 85701 285 2

Printed and bound in China

Royalties from this book will be donated to the charity SAFE!
Support for Young People Affected by Crime (www.safeproject.org.uk).

Acknowledgements: Sughra Bibi, Anne Whitehead, Chelsey Wilson, Ben
Lovatt, Alan Buckley, Emmy O'Shaughnessy, Jo Brown, Gema Hadridge, Mat
Lister, Marian Liebmann, Maya Kapsokavadis, Ruth Archer, Tikki Harrold,
pupils of Matthew Arnold School, Helen Austin, Tim Parkhouse, Chloe Purcell,
W.F. Southall Trust, Zahra Tehrani and the girls at the Young Women's Music
Project, Lisa Clark, Jessica Kingsley, Victoria Peters and everyone at JKP.

What Does Consent Really Mean?

Written by Pete Wallis and
Thalia Wallis

Illustrated by Joseph Wilkins

SINGING
DRAGON

London and Philadelphia

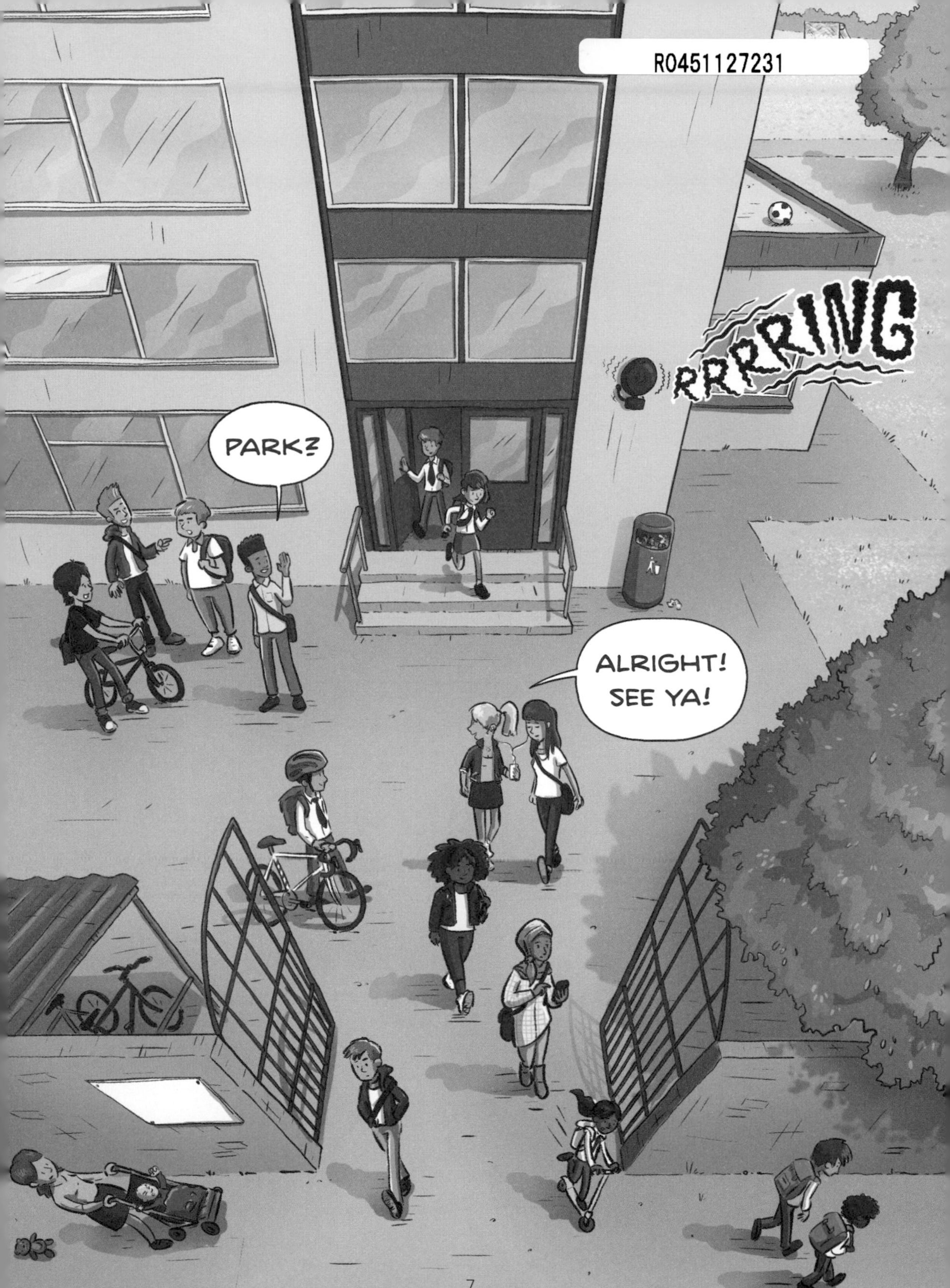
RRRRING
PARK?
ALRIGHT! SEE YA!

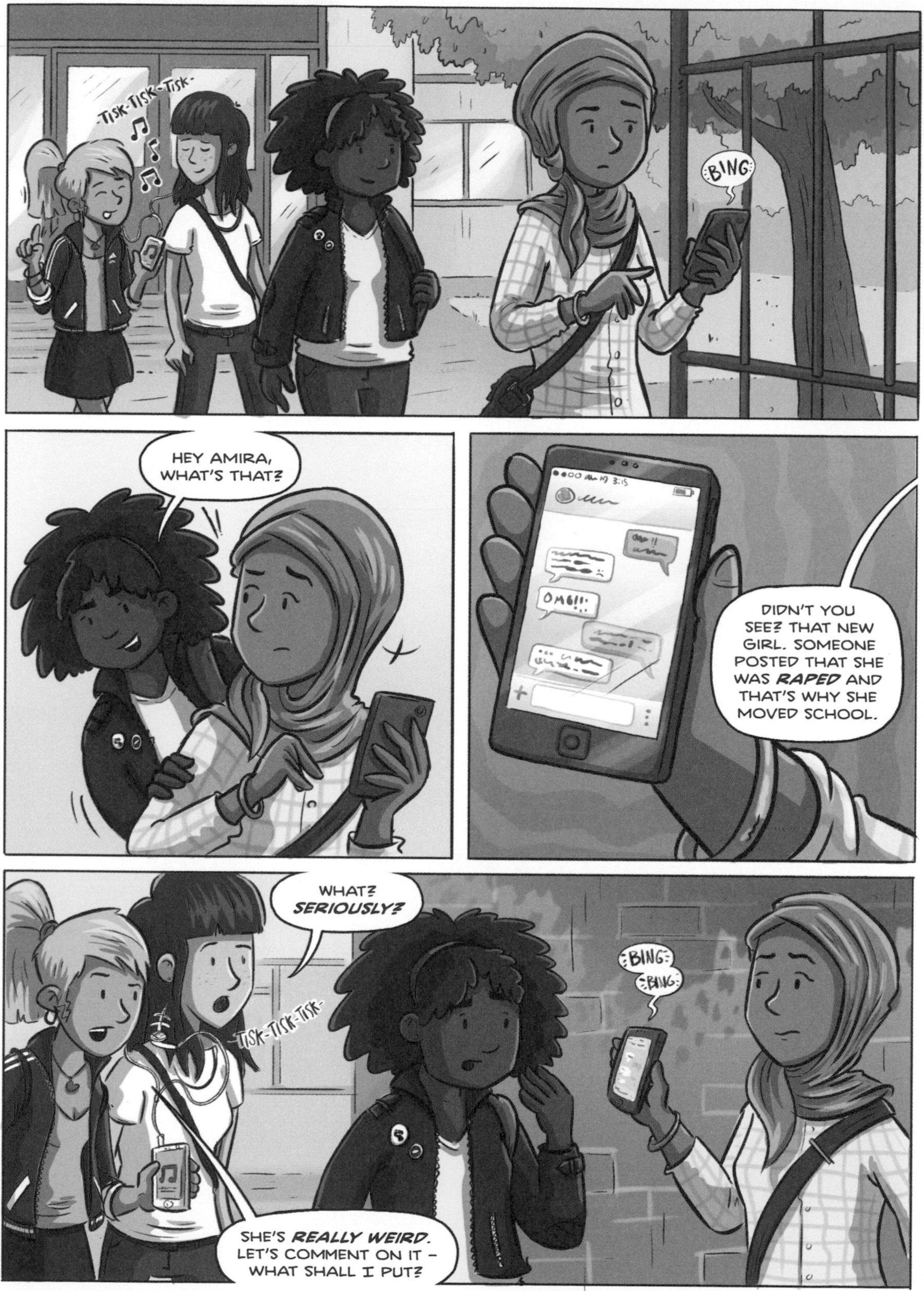

-TISK-TISK-TISK-
BING
HEY AMIRA, WHAT'S THAT?
OMG!!
DIDN'T YOU SEE? THAT NEW GIRL. SOMEONE POSTED THAT SHE WAS *RAPED* AND THAT'S WHY SHE MOVED SCHOOL.
WHAT? *SERIOUSLY?*
BING
BING
-TISK-TISK-TISK-
SHE'S *REALLY WEIRD*. LET'S COMMENT ON IT – WHAT SHALL I PUT?

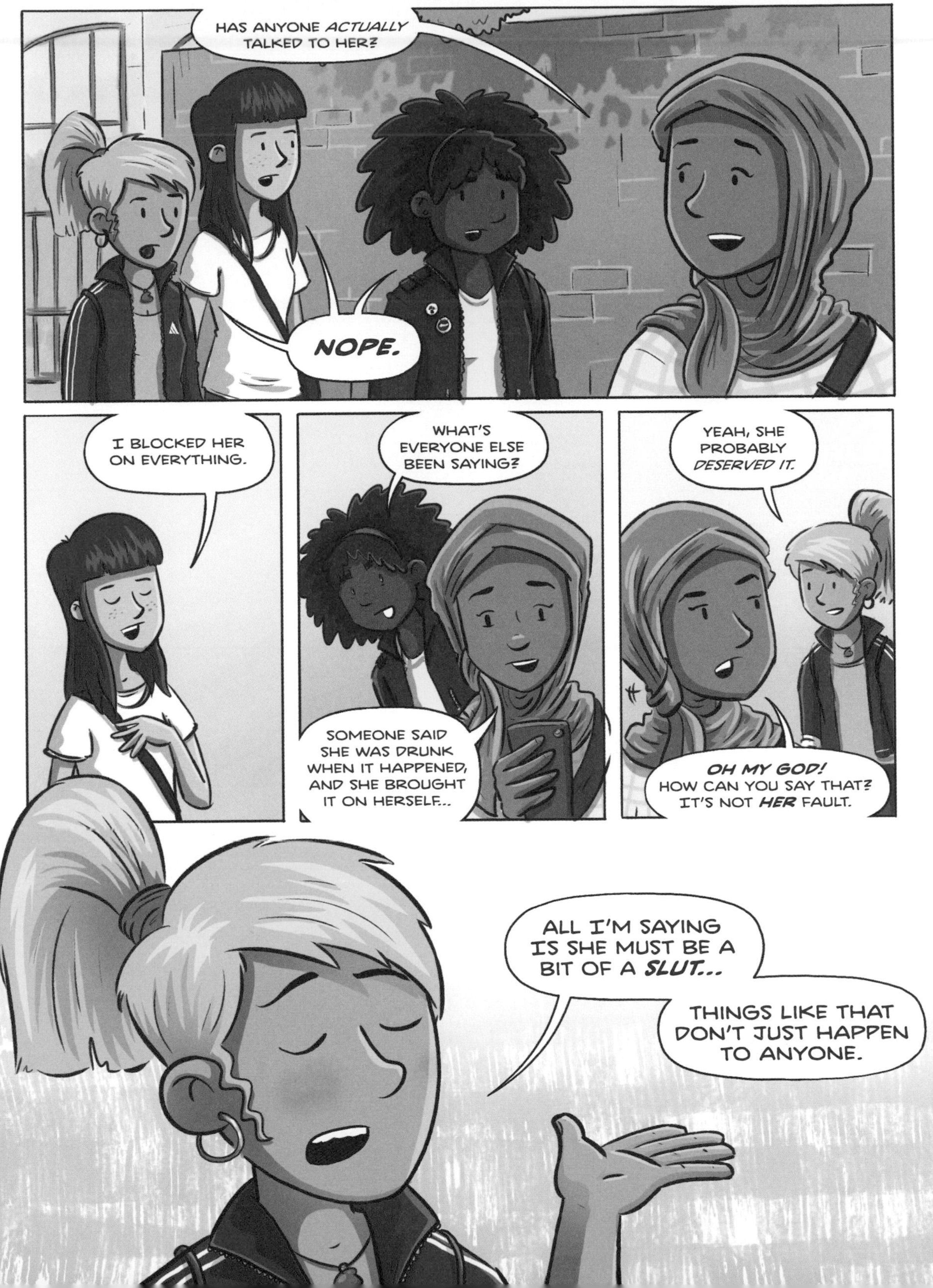
HAS ANYONE ACTUALLY TALKED TO HER?
NOPE.
I BLOCKED HER ON EVERYTHING.
WHAT'S EVERYONE ELSE BEEN SAYING?
SOMEONE SAID SHE WAS DRUNK WHEN IT HAPPENED, AND SHE BROUGHT IT ON HERSELF...
YEAH, SHE PROBABLY DESERVED IT.
OH MY GOD! HOW CAN YOU SAY THAT? IT'S NOT HER FAULT.
ALL I'M SAYING IS SHE MUST BE A BIT OF A SLUT...
THINGS LIKE THAT DON'T JUST HAPPEN TO ANYONE.

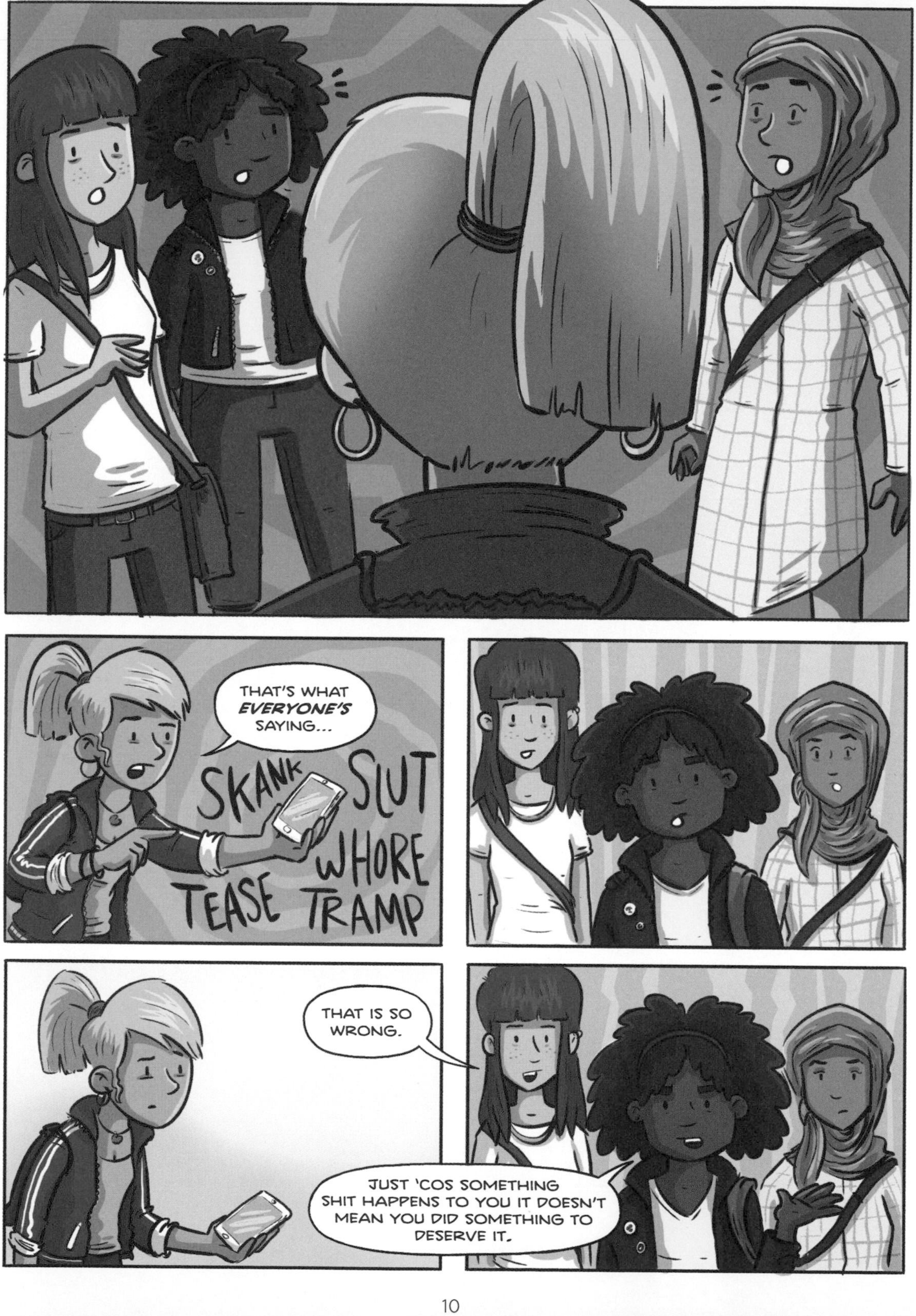
THAT'S WHAT *EVERYONE'S* SAYING...
SKANK
SLUT
WHORE
TEASE
TRAMP
THAT IS SO WRONG.
JUST 'COS SOMETHING SHIT HAPPENS TO YOU IT DOESN'T MEAN YOU DID SOMETHING TO DESERVE IT.

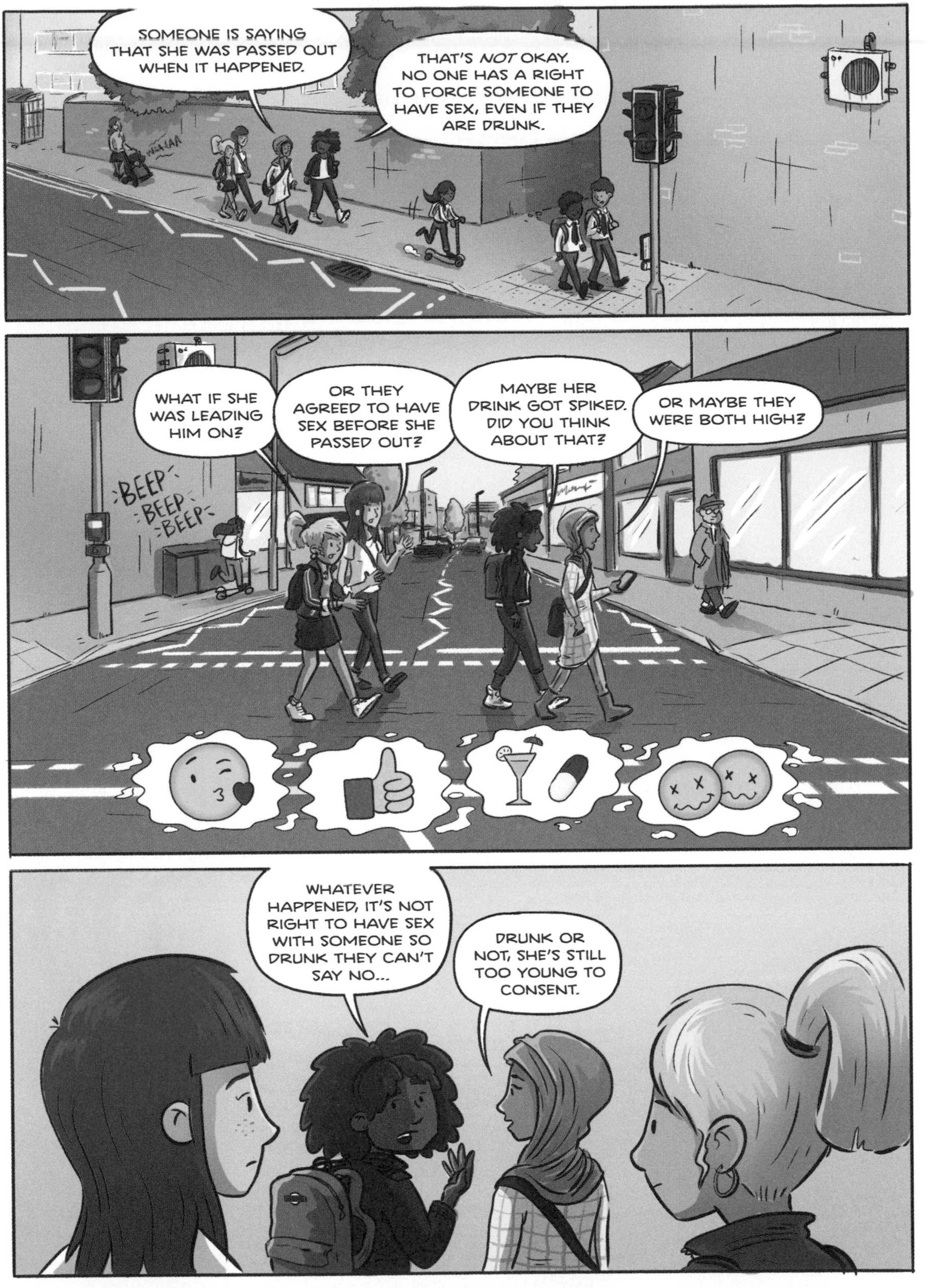
SOMEONE IS SAYING THAT SHE WAS PASSED OUT WHEN IT HAPPENED.
THAT'S *NOT* OKAY. NO ONE HAS A RIGHT TO FORCE SOMEONE TO HAVE SEX, EVEN IF THEY ARE DRUNK.
WAAAA
WHAT IF SHE WAS LEADING HIM ON?
OR THEY AGREED TO HAVE SEX BEFORE SHE PASSED OUT?
MAYBE HER DRINK GOT SPIKED. DID YOU THINK ABOUT THAT?
OR MAYBE THEY WERE BOTH HIGH?
BEEP BEEP BEEP
WHATEVER HAPPENED, IT'S NOT RIGHT TO HAVE SEX WITH SOMEONE SO DRUNK THEY CAN'T SAY NO...
DRUNK OR NOT, SHE'S STILL TOO YOUNG TO CONSENT.

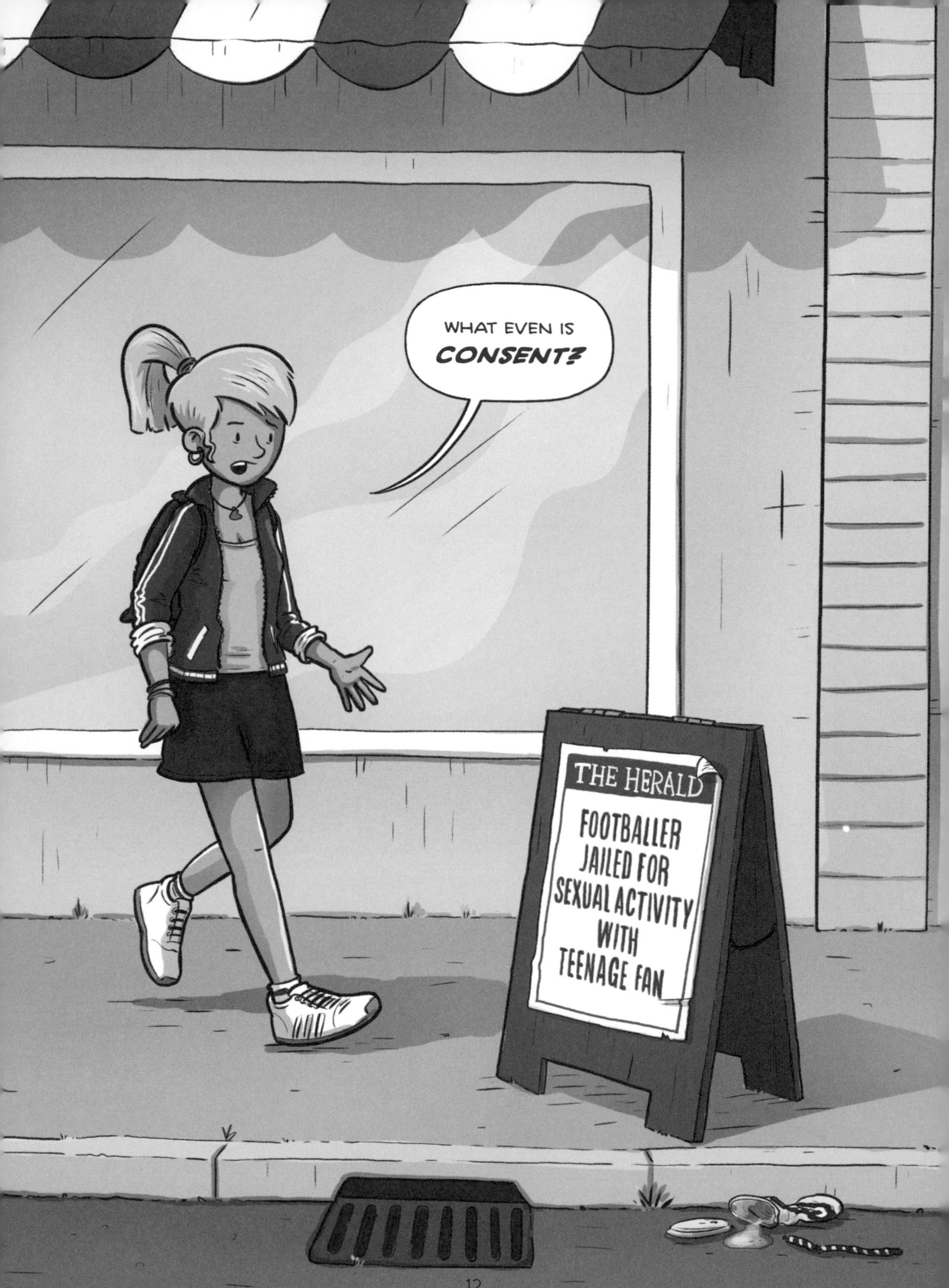
WHAT EVEN IS CONSENT?
THE HERALD
FOOTBALLER JAILED FOR SEXUAL ACTIVITY WITH TEENAGE FAN

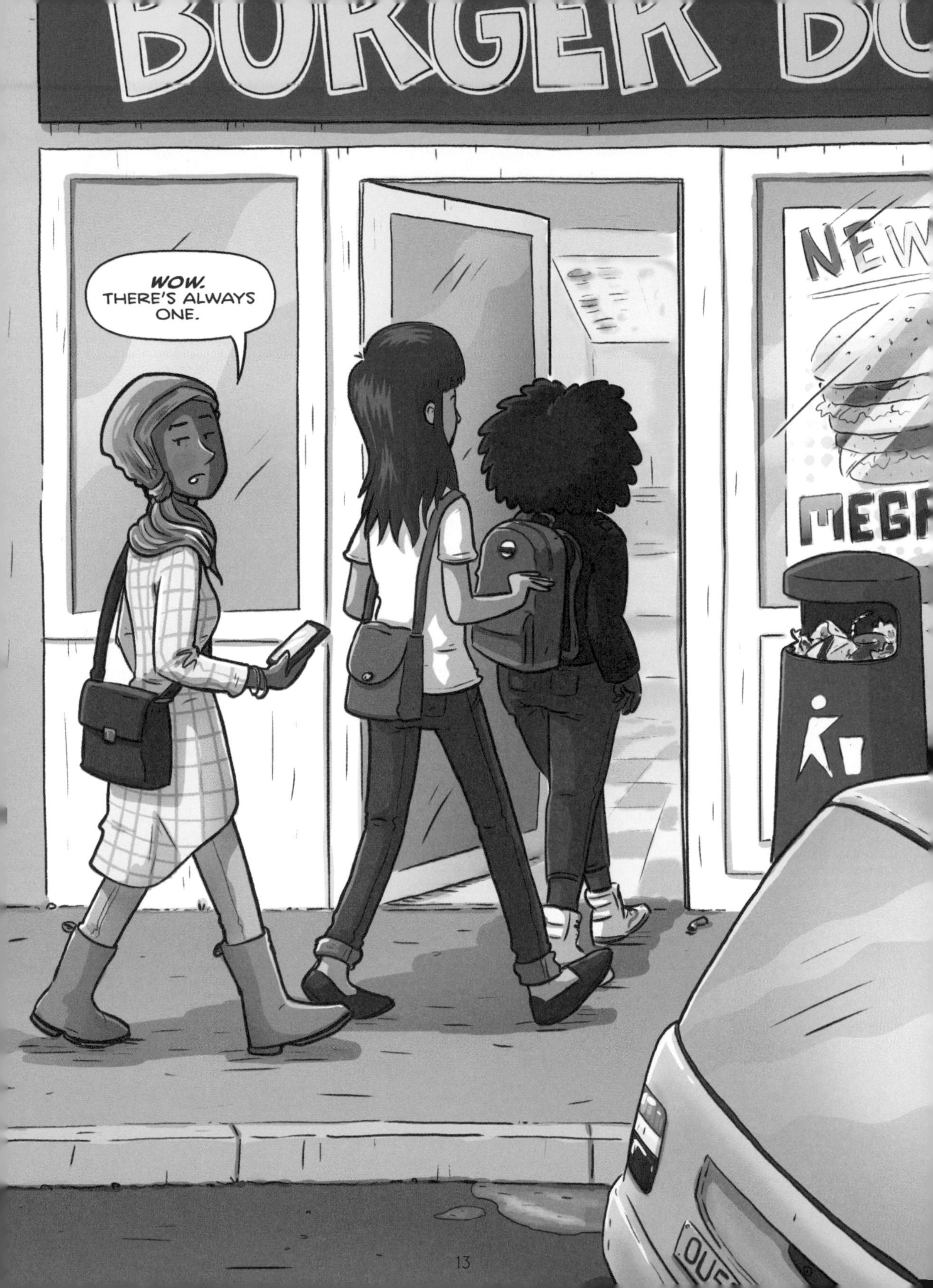
BURGER B
WOW. THERE'S ALWAYS ONE.
NEW
MEGA

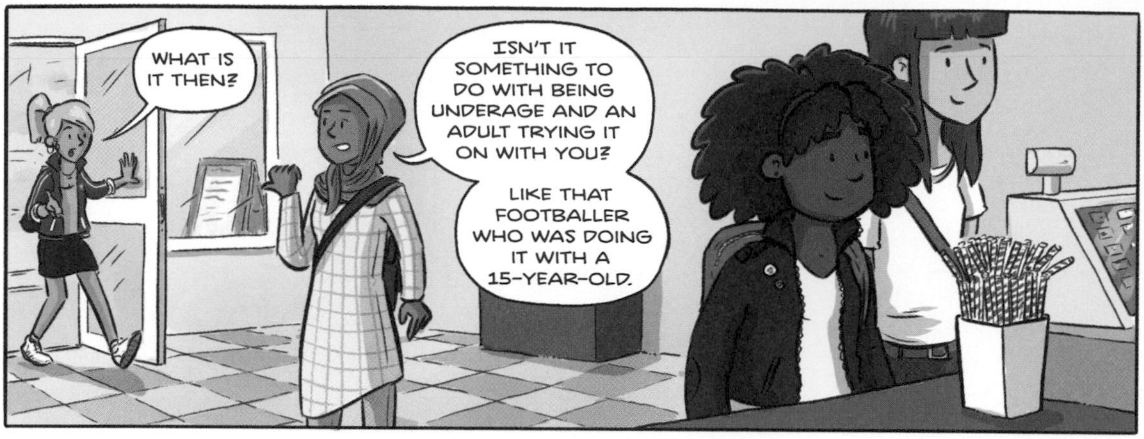
WHAT IS IT THEN?
ISN'T IT SOMETHING TO DO WITH BEING UNDERAGE AND AN ADULT TRYING IT ON WITH YOU?
LIKE THAT FOOTBALLER WHO WAS DOING IT WITH A 15-YEAR-OLD.

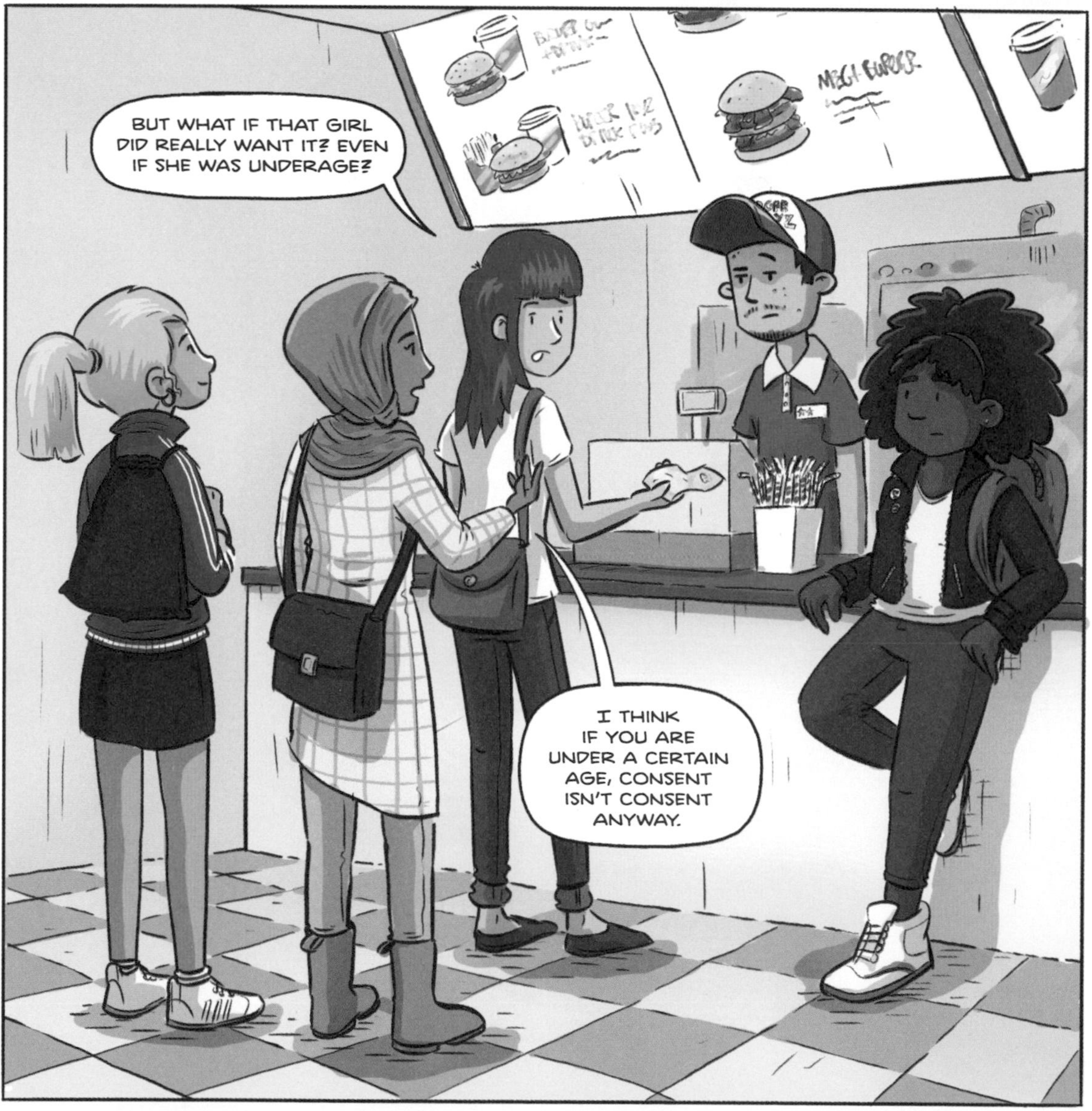
BUT WHAT IF THAT GIRL DID REALLY WANT IT? EVEN IF SHE WAS UNDERAGE?
I THINK IF YOU ARE UNDER A CERTAIN AGE, CONSENT ISN'T CONSENT ANYWAY.

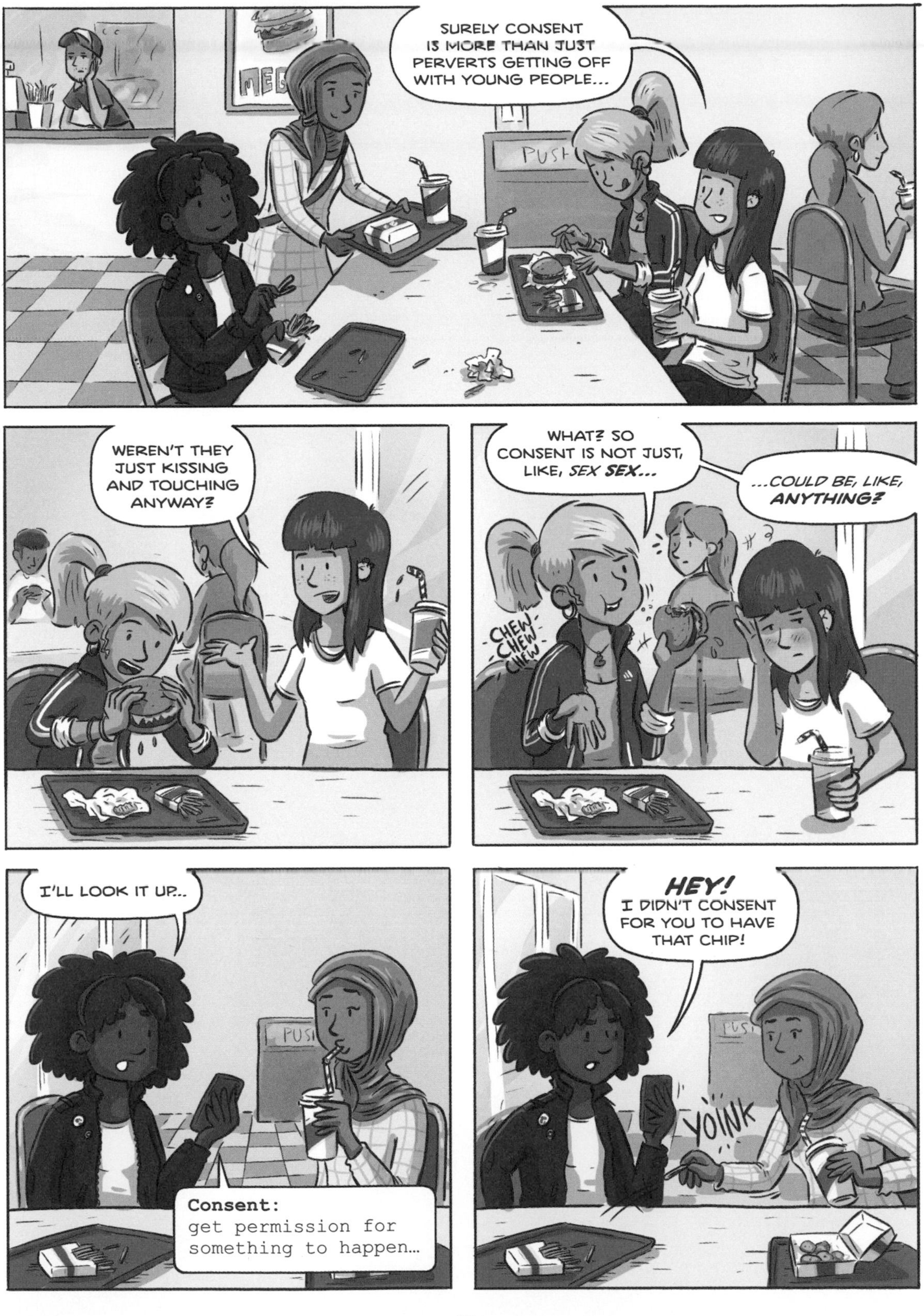
SURELY CONSENT IS MORE THAN JUST PERVERTS GETTING OFF WITH YOUNG PEOPLE...
PUSH
WEREN'T THEY JUST KISSING AND TOUCHING ANYWAY?
WHAT? SO CONSENT IS NOT JUST, LIKE, *SEX* ***SEX...***
...COULD BE, LIKE, ***ANYTHING?***
CHEW CHEW CHEW
I'LL LOOK IT UP...
Consent:
get permission for something to happen...
HEY!
I DIDN'T CONSENT FOR YOU TO HAVE THAT CHIP!
YOINK

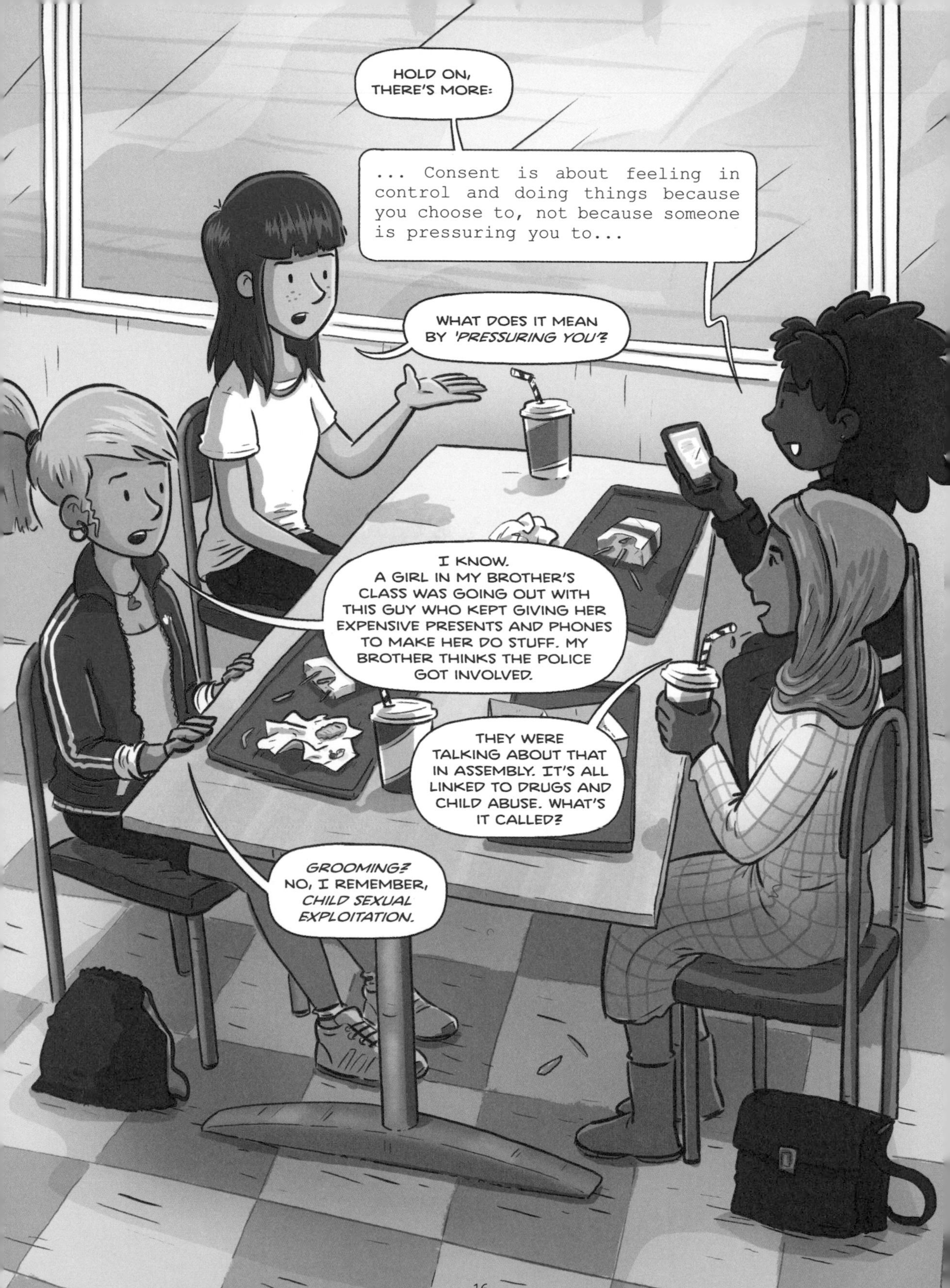
HOLD ON, THERE'S MORE:
... Consent is about feeling in control and doing things because you choose to, not because someone is pressuring you to...
WHAT DOES IT MEAN BY 'PRESSURING YOU'?
I KNOW. A GIRL IN MY BROTHER'S CLASS WAS GOING OUT WITH THIS GUY WHO KEPT GIVING HER EXPENSIVE PRESENTS AND PHONES TO MAKE HER DO STUFF. MY BROTHER THINKS THE POLICE GOT INVOLVED.
THEY WERE TALKING ABOUT THAT IN ASSEMBLY. IT'S ALL LINKED TO DRUGS AND CHILD ABUSE. WHAT'S IT CALLED?
GROOMING? NO, I REMEMBER, CHILD SEXUAL EXPLOITATION.

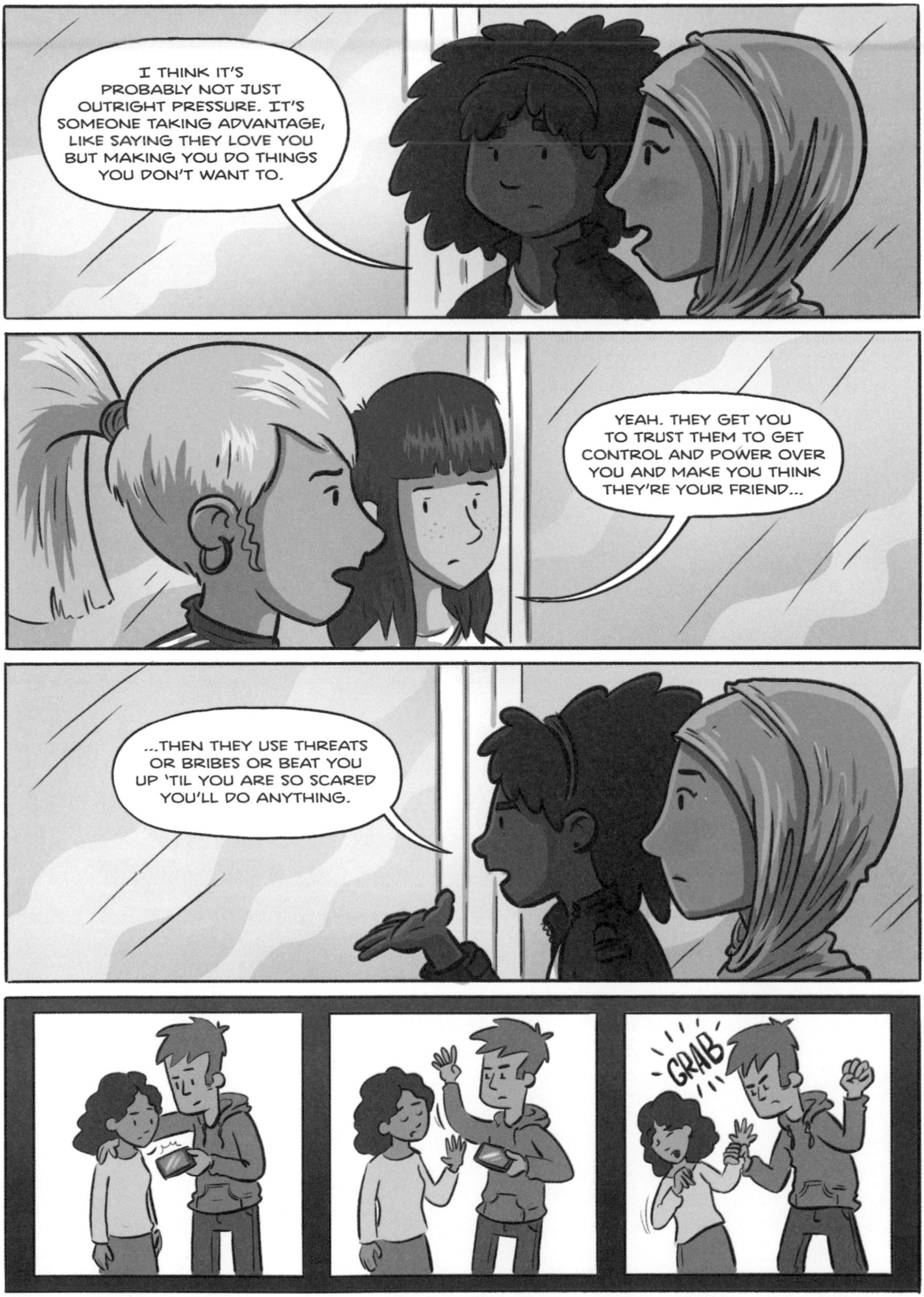
I THINK IT'S PROBABLY NOT JUST OUTRIGHT PRESSURE. IT'S SOMEONE TAKING ADVANTAGE, LIKE SAYING THEY LOVE YOU BUT MAKING YOU DO THINGS YOU DON'T WANT TO.
YEAH. THEY GET YOU TO TRUST THEM TO GET CONTROL AND POWER OVER YOU AND MAKE YOU THINK THEY'RE YOUR FRIEND...
...THEN THEY USE THREATS OR BRIBES OR BEAT YOU UP 'TIL YOU ARE SO SCARED YOU'LL DO ANYTHING.
GRAB

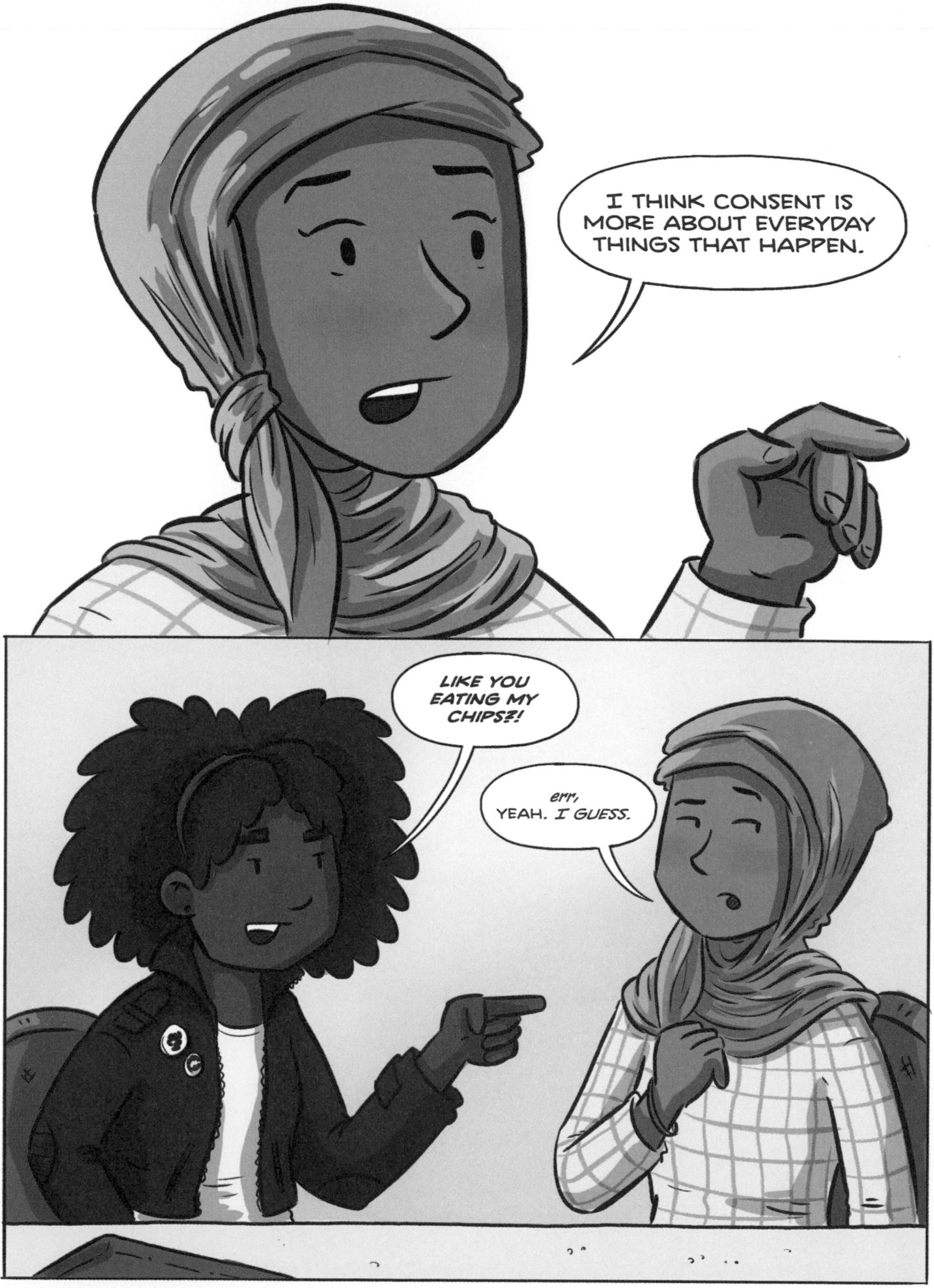
I THINK CONSENT IS MORE ABOUT EVERYDAY THINGS THAT HAPPEN.
LIKE YOU EATING MY CHIPS?!
err, YEAH. I GUESS.

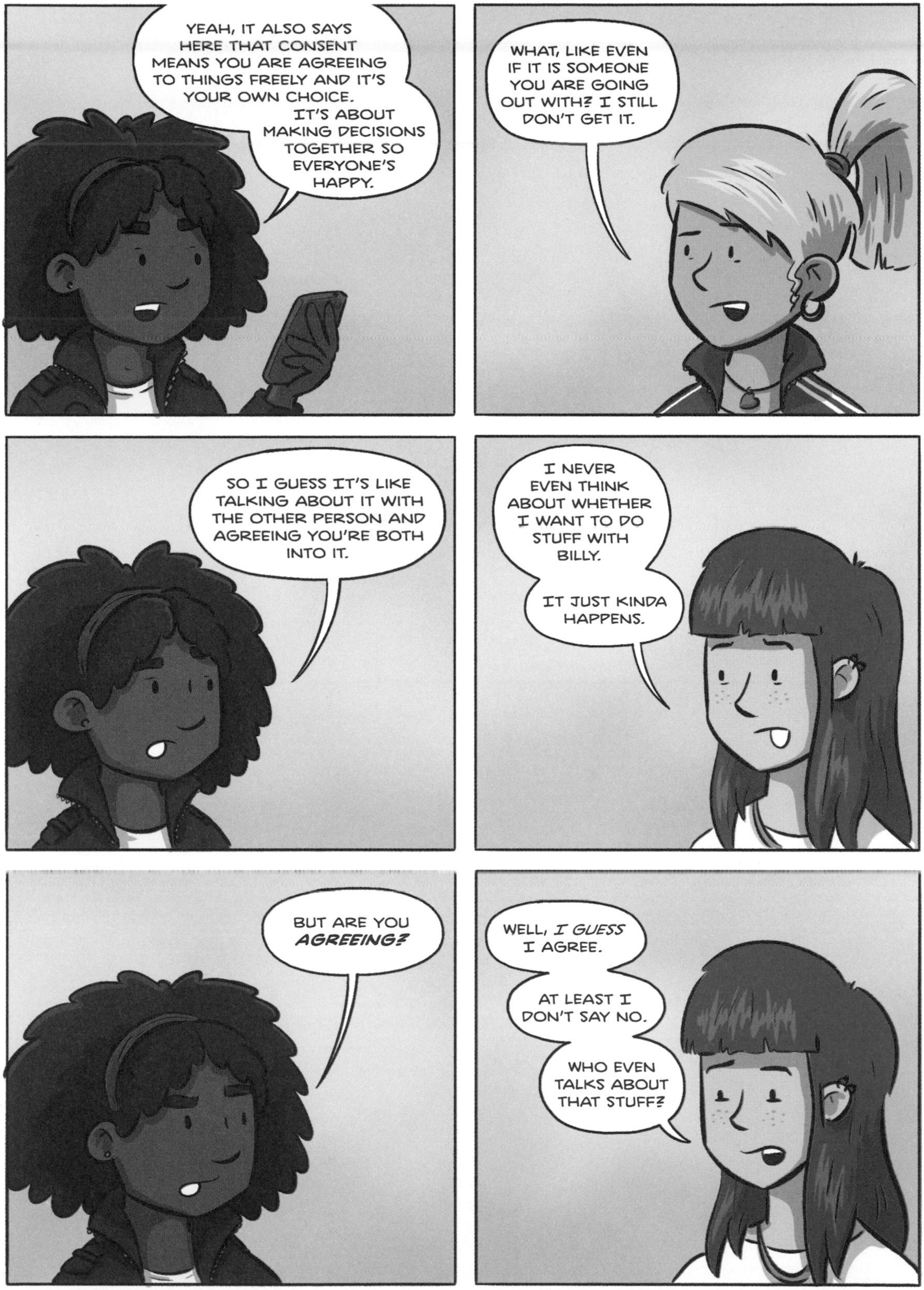
YEAH, IT ALSO SAYS HERE THAT CONSENT MEANS YOU ARE AGREEING TO THINGS FREELY AND IT'S YOUR OWN CHOICE.
IT'S ABOUT MAKING DECISIONS TOGETHER SO EVERYONE'S HAPPY.
WHAT, LIKE EVEN IF IT IS SOMEONE YOU ARE GOING OUT WITH? I STILL DON'T GET IT.
SO I GUESS IT'S LIKE TALKING ABOUT IT WITH THE OTHER PERSON AND AGREEING YOU'RE BOTH INTO IT.
I NEVER EVEN THINK ABOUT WHETHER I WANT TO DO STUFF WITH BILLY.
IT JUST KINDA HAPPENS.
BUT ARE YOU ***AGREEING?***
WELL, *I GUESS* I AGREE.
AT LEAST I DON'T SAY NO.
WHO EVEN TALKS ABOUT THAT STUFF?

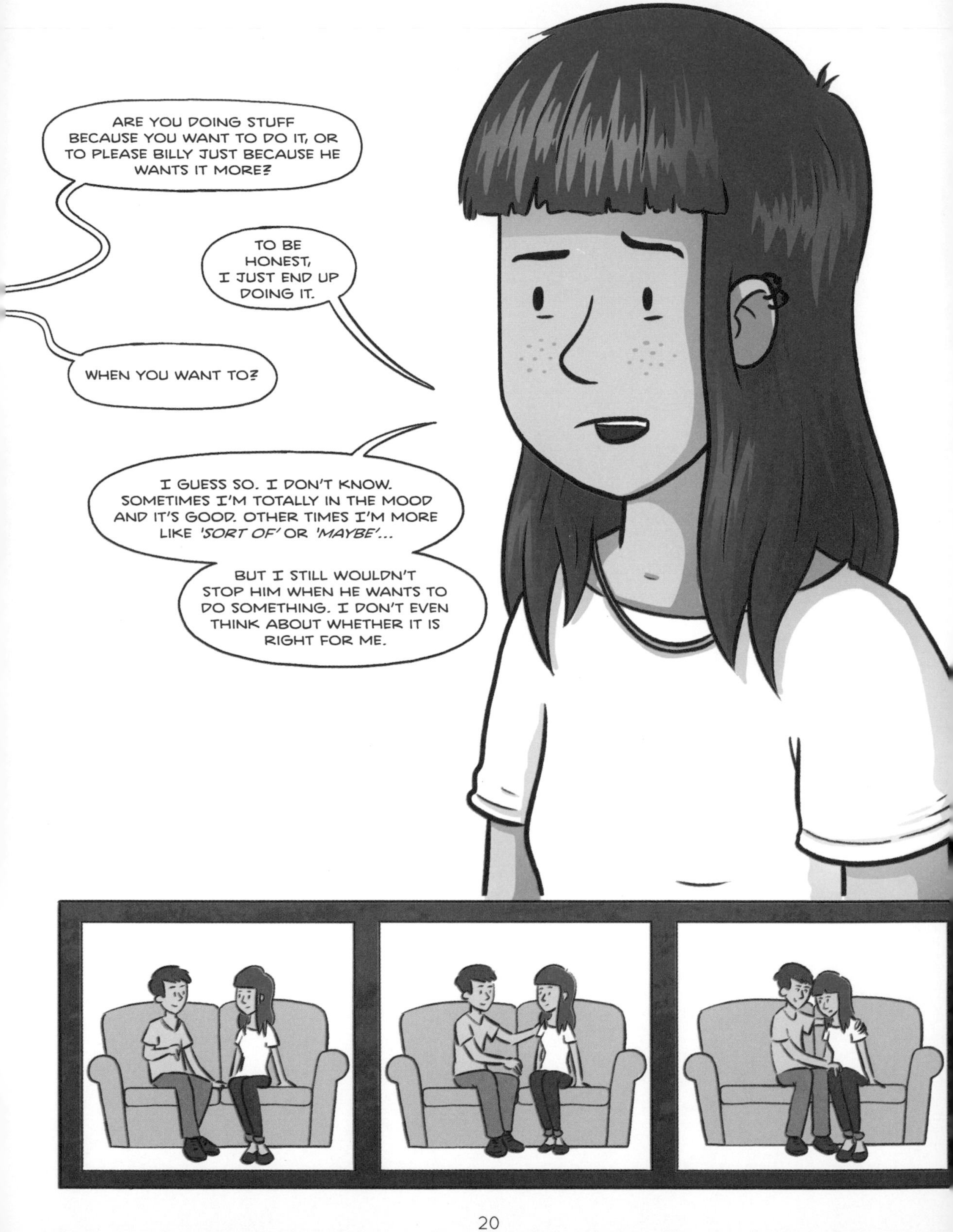
ARE YOU DOING STUFF BECAUSE YOU WANT TO DO IT, OR TO PLEASE BILLY JUST BECAUSE HE WANTS IT MORE?
TO BE HONEST, I JUST END UP DOING IT.
WHEN YOU WANT TO?
I GUESS SO. I DON'T KNOW. SOMETIMES I'M TOTALLY IN THE MOOD AND IT'S GOOD. OTHER TIMES I'M MORE LIKE *'SORT OF'* OR *'MAYBE'*...
BUT I STILL WOULDN'T STOP HIM WHEN HE WANTS TO DO SOMETHING. I DON'T EVEN THINK ABOUT WHETHER IT IS RIGHT FOR ME.

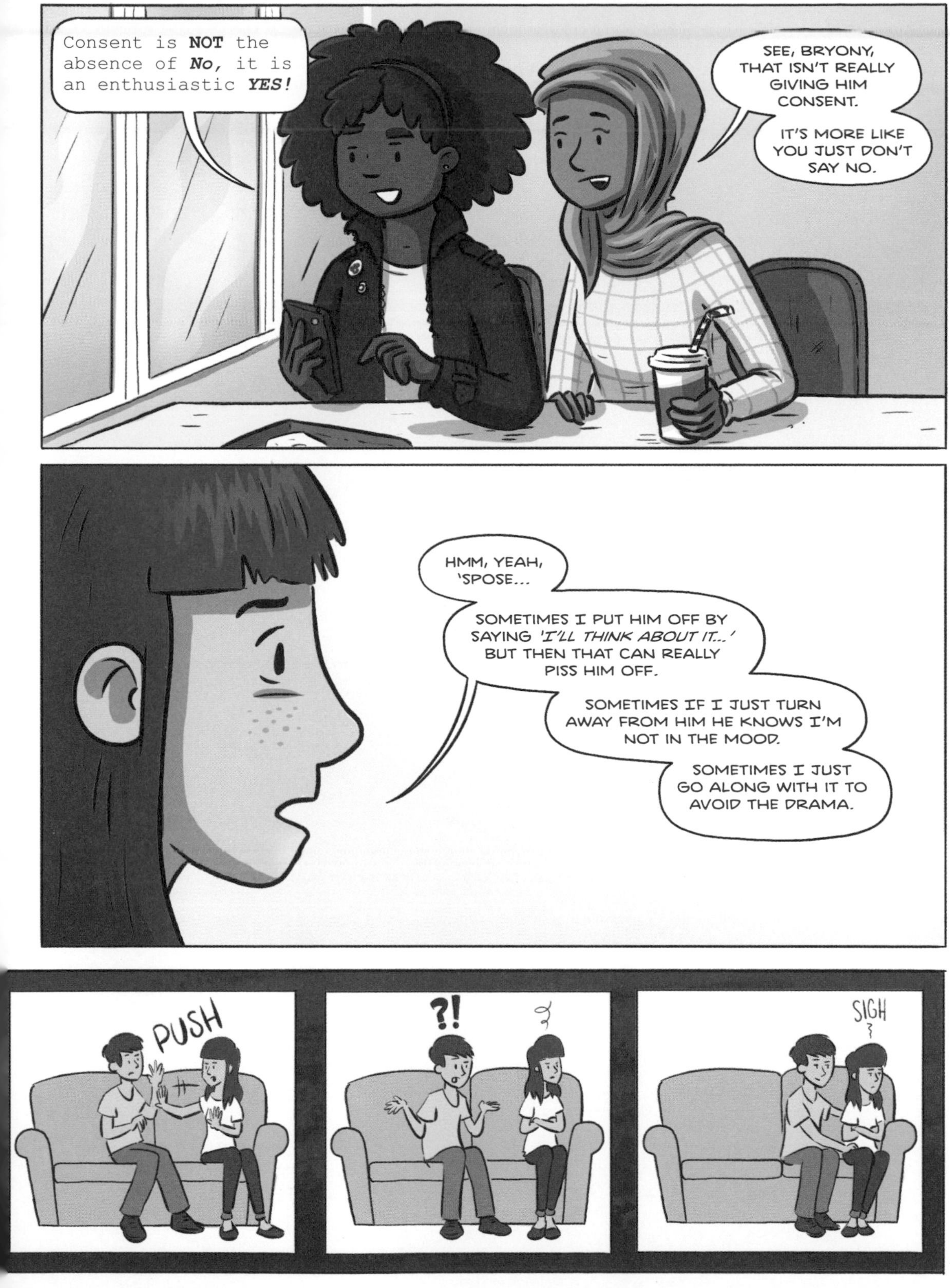
Consent is **NOT** the absence of ***No***, it is an enthusiastic ***YES!***
SEE, BRYONY, THAT ISN'T REALLY GIVING HIM CONSENT.
IT'S MORE LIKE YOU JUST DON'T SAY NO.
HMM, YEAH, 'SPOSE...
SOMETIMES I PUT HIM OFF BY SAYING *'I'LL THINK ABOUT IT...'* BUT THEN THAT CAN REALLY PISS HIM OFF.
SOMETIMES IF I JUST TURN AWAY FROM HIM HE KNOWS I'M NOT IN THE MOOD.
SOMETIMES I JUST GO ALONG WITH IT TO AVOID THE DRAMA.
PUSH
?!
SIGH

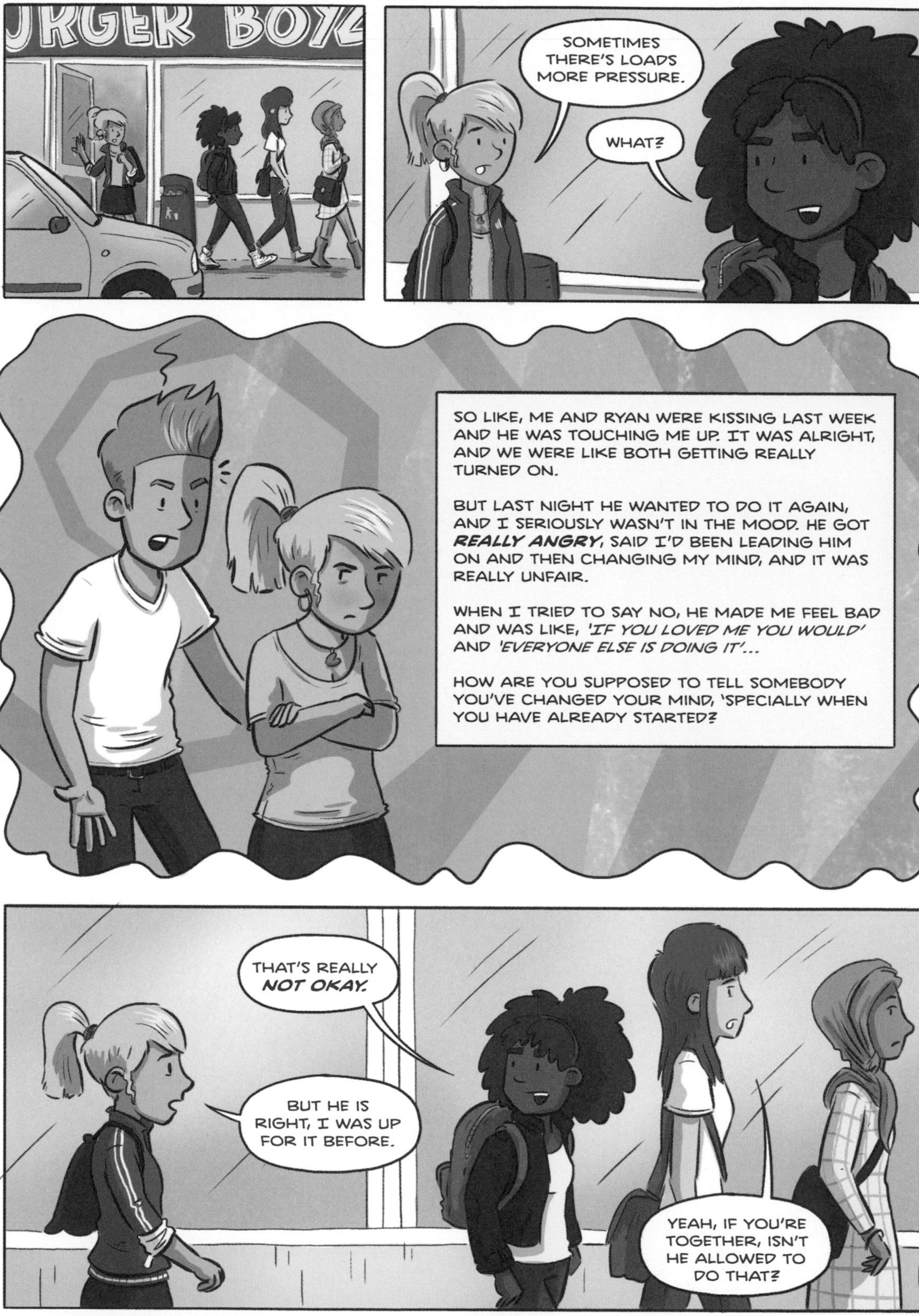
URGER BOYZ
SOMETIMES THERE'S LOADS MORE PRESSURE.
WHAT?
SO LIKE, ME AND RYAN WERE KISSING LAST WEEK AND HE WAS TOUCHING ME UP. IT WAS ALRIGHT, AND WE WERE LIKE BOTH GETTING REALLY TURNED ON.
BUT LAST NIGHT HE WANTED TO DO IT AGAIN, AND I SERIOUSLY WASN'T IN THE MOOD. HE GOT ***REALLY ANGRY***, SAID I'D BEEN LEADING HIM ON AND THEN CHANGING MY MIND, AND IT WAS REALLY UNFAIR.
WHEN I TRIED TO SAY NO, HE MADE ME FEEL BAD AND WAS LIKE, *'IF YOU LOVED ME YOU WOULD'* AND *'EVERYONE ELSE IS DOING IT'...*
HOW ARE YOU SUPPOSED TO TELL SOMEBODY YOU'VE CHANGED YOUR MIND, 'SPECIALLY WHEN YOU HAVE ALREADY STARTED?
THAT'S REALLY ***NOT OKAY.***
BUT HE IS RIGHT, I WAS UP FOR IT BEFORE.
YEAH, IF YOU'RE TOGETHER, ISN'T HE ALLOWED TO DO THAT?

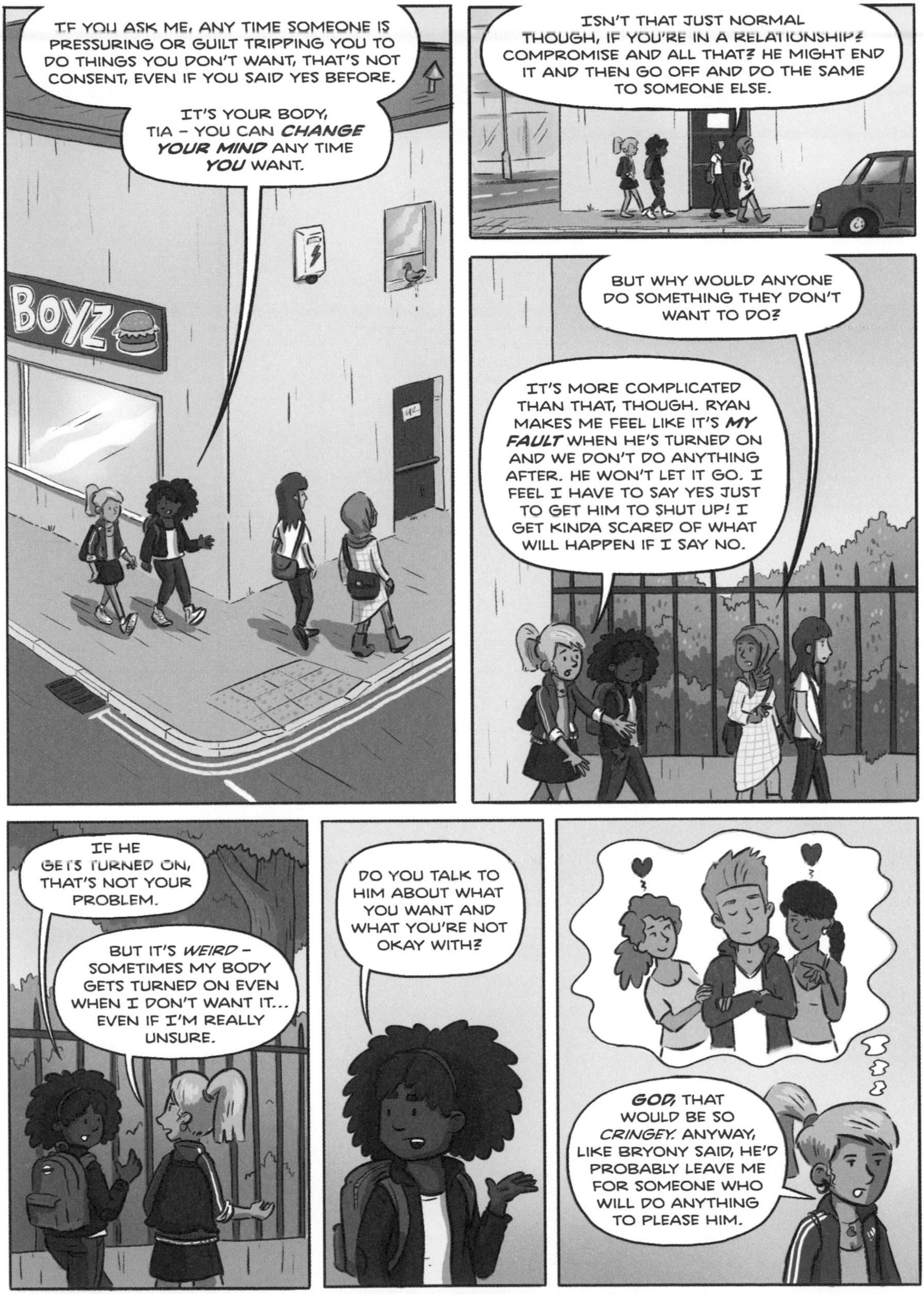
IF YOU ASK ME, ANY TIME SOMEONE IS PRESSURING OR GUILT TRIPPING YOU TO DO THINGS YOU DON'T WANT, THAT'S NOT CONSENT, EVEN IF YOU SAID YES BEFORE.
IT'S YOUR BODY, TIA – YOU CAN *CHANGE YOUR MIND* ANY TIME *YOU* WANT.
BOYZ
ISN'T THAT JUST NORMAL THOUGH, IF YOU'RE IN A RELATIONSHIP? COMPROMISE AND ALL THAT? HE MIGHT END IT AND THEN GO OFF AND DO THE SAME TO SOMEONE ELSE.
BUT WHY WOULD ANYONE DO SOMETHING THEY DON'T WANT TO DO?
IT'S MORE COMPLICATED THAN THAT, THOUGH. RYAN MAKES ME FEEL LIKE IT'S *MY FAULT* WHEN HE'S TURNED ON AND WE DON'T DO ANYTHING AFTER. HE WON'T LET IT GO. I FEEL I HAVE TO SAY YES JUST TO GET HIM TO SHUT UP! I GET KINDA SCARED OF WHAT WILL HAPPEN IF I SAY NO.
IF HE GETS TURNED ON, THAT'S NOT YOUR PROBLEM.
BUT IT'S *WEIRD* – SOMETIMES MY BODY GETS TURNED ON EVEN WHEN I DON'T WANT IT... EVEN IF I'M REALLY UNSURE.
DO YOU TALK TO HIM ABOUT WHAT YOU WANT AND WHAT YOU'RE NOT OKAY WITH?
GOD, THAT WOULD BE SO *CRINGEY*. ANYWAY, LIKE BRYONY SAID, HE'D PROBABLY LEAVE ME FOR SOMEONE WHO WILL DO ANYTHING TO PLEASE HIM.

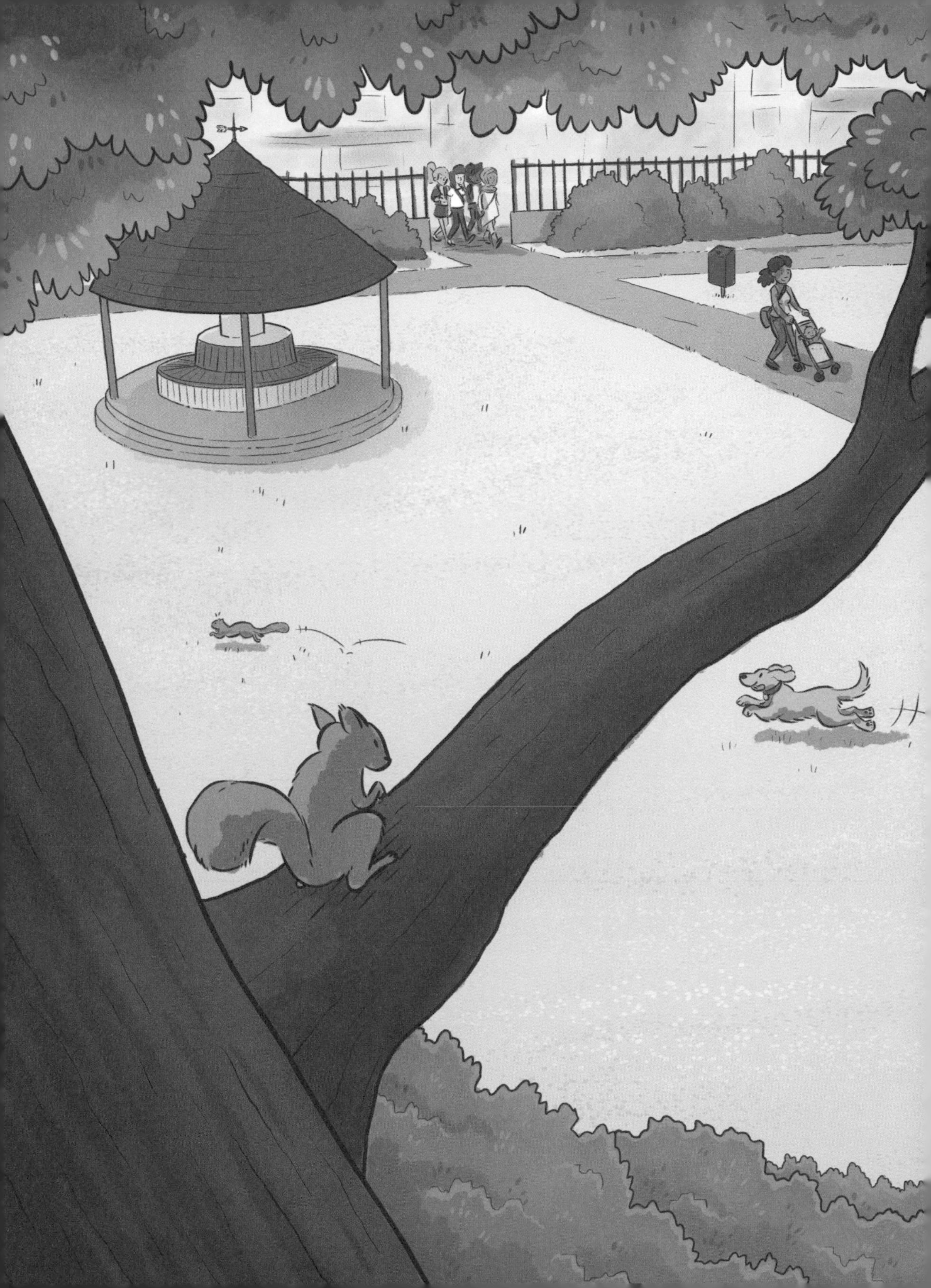

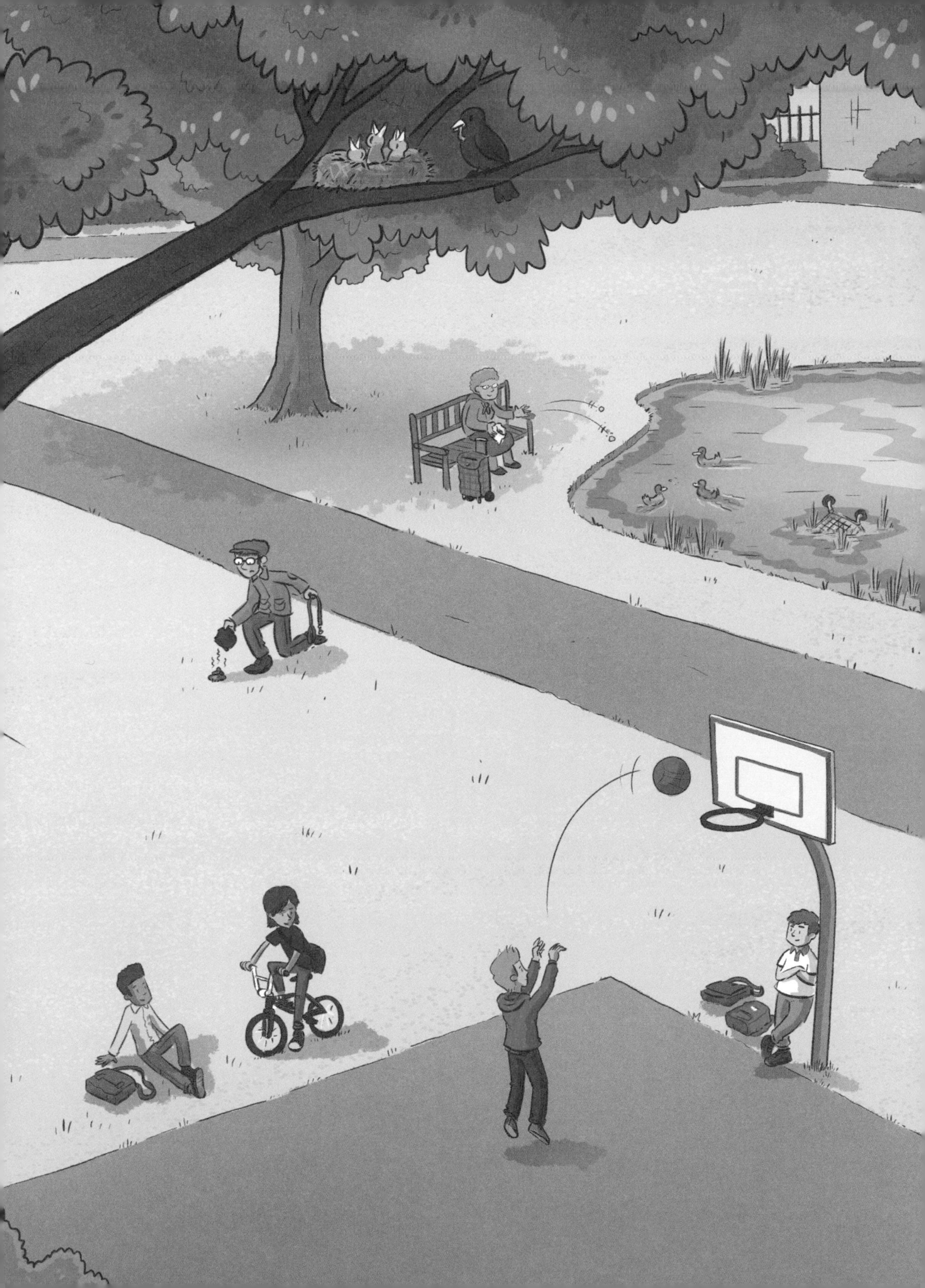

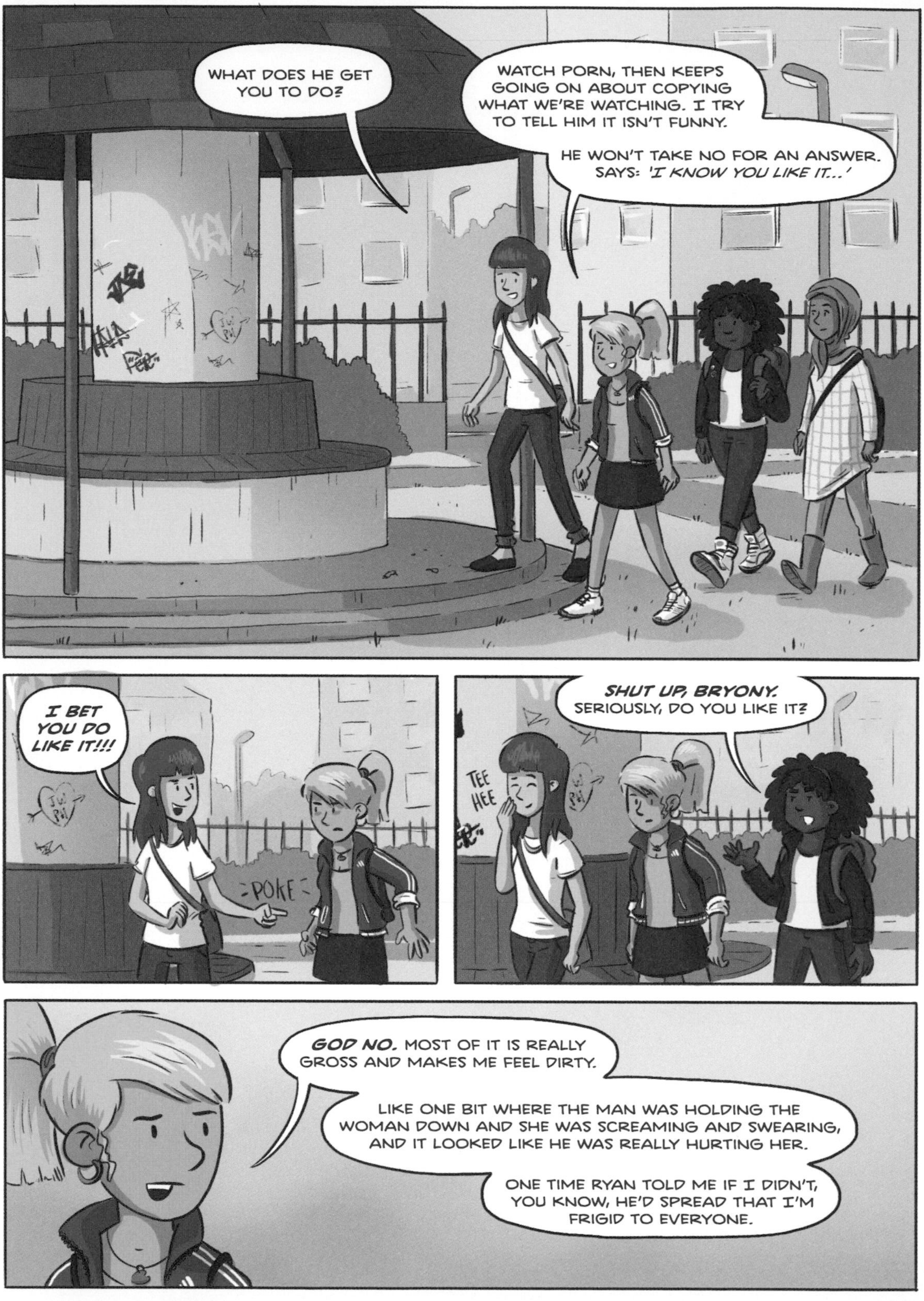
WHAT DOES HE GET YOU TO DO?
WATCH PORN, THEN KEEPS GOING ON ABOUT COPYING WHAT WE'RE WATCHING. I TRY TO TELL HIM IT ISN'T FUNNY.
HE WON'T TAKE NO FOR AN ANSWER. SAYS: *'I KNOW YOU LIKE IT...'*
I BET YOU DO LIKE IT!!!
POKE
TEE HEE
SHUT UP, BRYONY. SERIOUSLY, DO YOU LIKE IT?
GOD NO. MOST OF IT IS REALLY GROSS AND MAKES ME FEEL DIRTY.
LIKE ONE BIT WHERE THE MAN WAS HOLDING THE WOMAN DOWN AND SHE WAS SCREAMING AND SWEARING, AND IT LOOKED LIKE HE WAS REALLY HURTING HER.
ONE TIME RYAN TOLD ME IF I DIDN'T, YOU KNOW, HE'D SPREAD THAT I'M FRIGID TO EVERYONE.

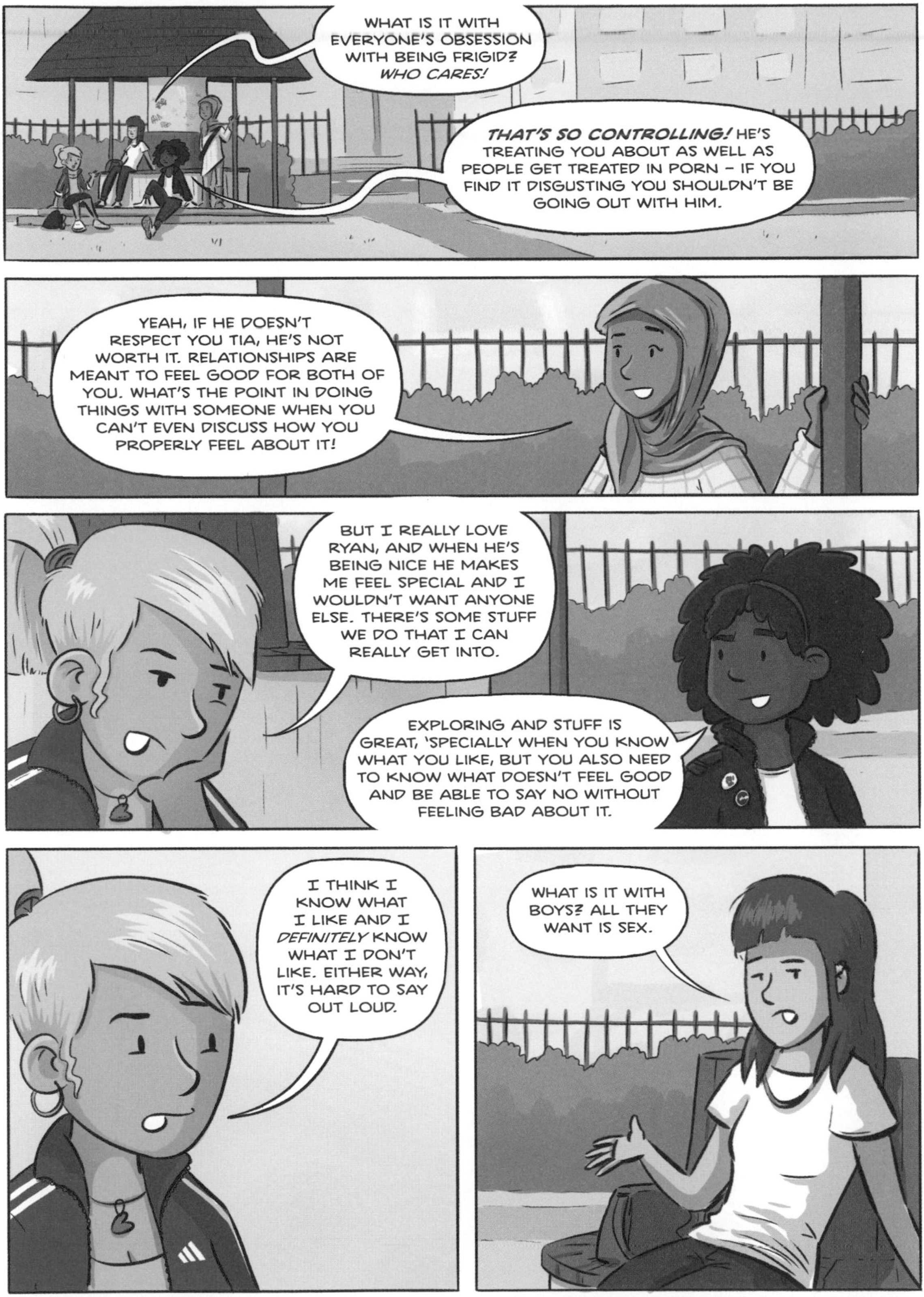
WHAT IS IT WITH EVERYONE'S OBSESSION WITH BEING FRIGID? *WHO CARES!*
THAT'S SO CONTROLLING! HE'S TREATING YOU ABOUT AS WELL AS PEOPLE GET TREATED IN PORN – IF YOU FIND IT DISGUSTING YOU SHOULDN'T BE GOING OUT WITH HIM.
YEAH, IF HE DOESN'T RESPECT YOU TIA, HE'S NOT WORTH IT. RELATIONSHIPS ARE MEANT TO FEEL GOOD FOR BOTH OF YOU. WHAT'S THE POINT IN DOING THINGS WITH SOMEONE WHEN YOU CAN'T EVEN DISCUSS HOW YOU PROPERLY FEEL ABOUT IT!
BUT I REALLY LOVE RYAN, AND WHEN HE'S BEING NICE HE MAKES ME FEEL SPECIAL AND I WOULDN'T WANT ANYONE ELSE. THERE'S SOME STUFF WE DO THAT I CAN REALLY GET INTO.
EXPLORING AND STUFF IS GREAT, 'SPECIALLY WHEN YOU KNOW WHAT YOU LIKE, BUT YOU ALSO NEED TO KNOW WHAT DOESN'T FEEL GOOD AND BE ABLE TO SAY NO WITHOUT FEELING BAD ABOUT IT.
I THINK I KNOW WHAT I LIKE AND I *DEFINITELY* KNOW WHAT I DON'T LIKE. EITHER WAY, IT'S HARD TO SAY OUT LOUD.
WHAT IS IT WITH BOYS? ALL THEY WANT IS SEX.

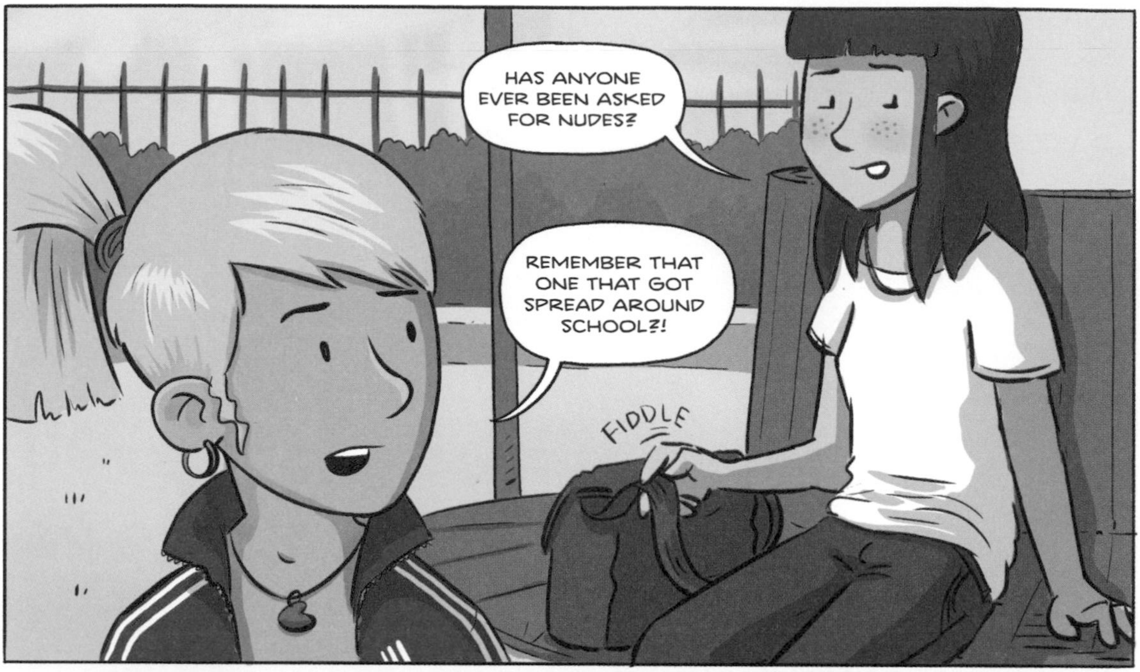
HAS ANYONE EVER BEEN ASKED FOR NUDES?
REMEMBER THAT ONE THAT GOT SPREAD AROUND SCHOOL?!
FIDDLE

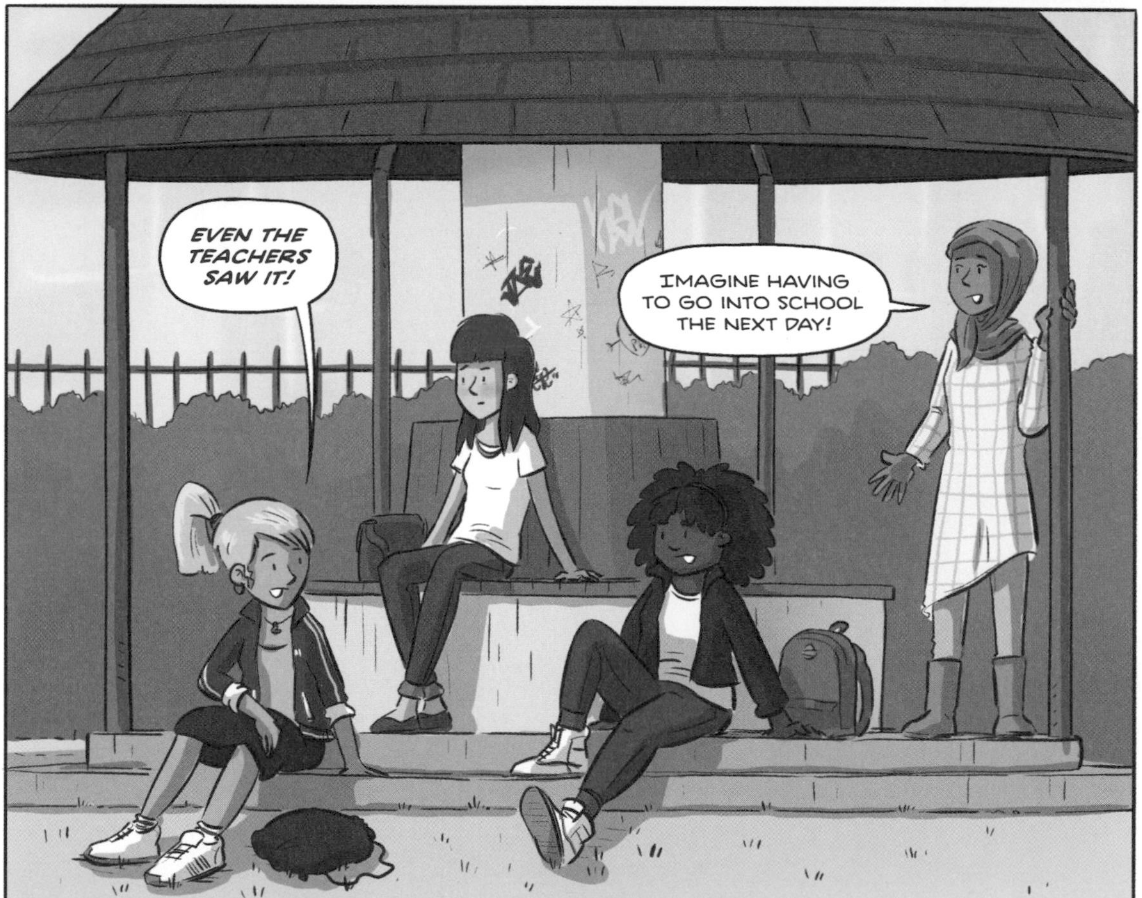
EVEN THE TEACHERS SAW IT!
IMAGINE HAVING TO GO INTO SCHOOL THE NEXT DAY!

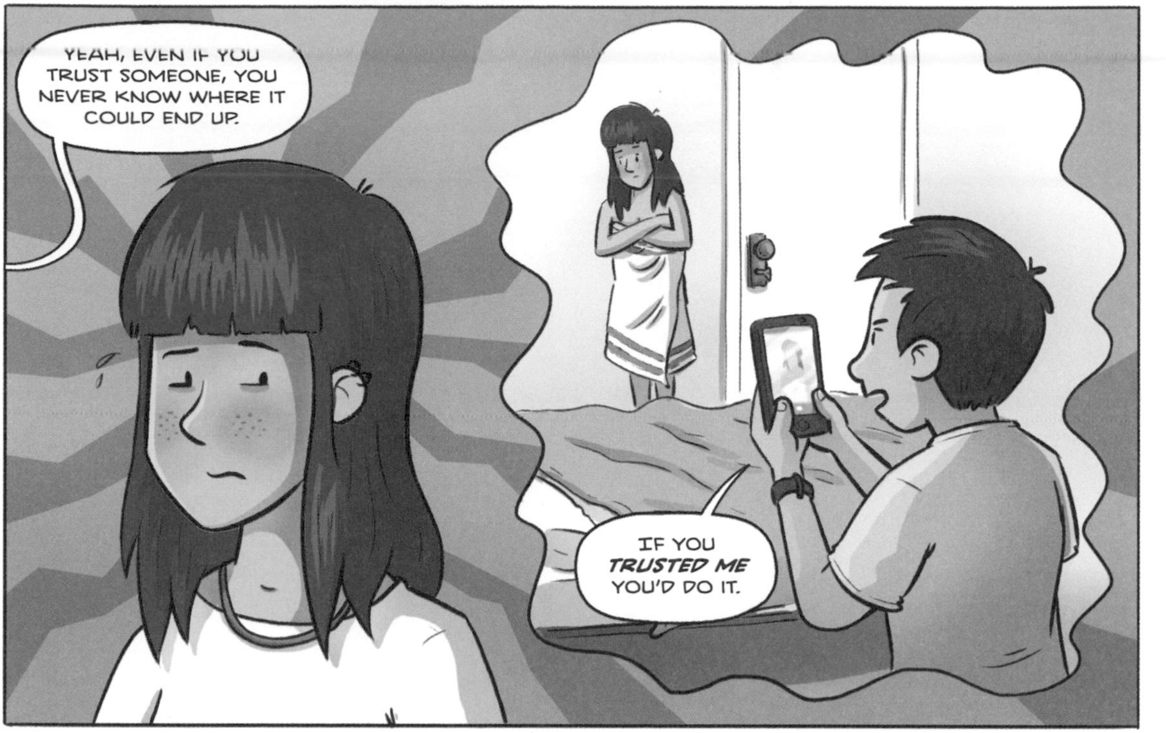
YEAH, EVEN IF YOU TRUST SOMEONE, YOU NEVER KNOW WHERE IT COULD END UP.
IF YOU *TRUSTED ME* YOU'D DO IT.

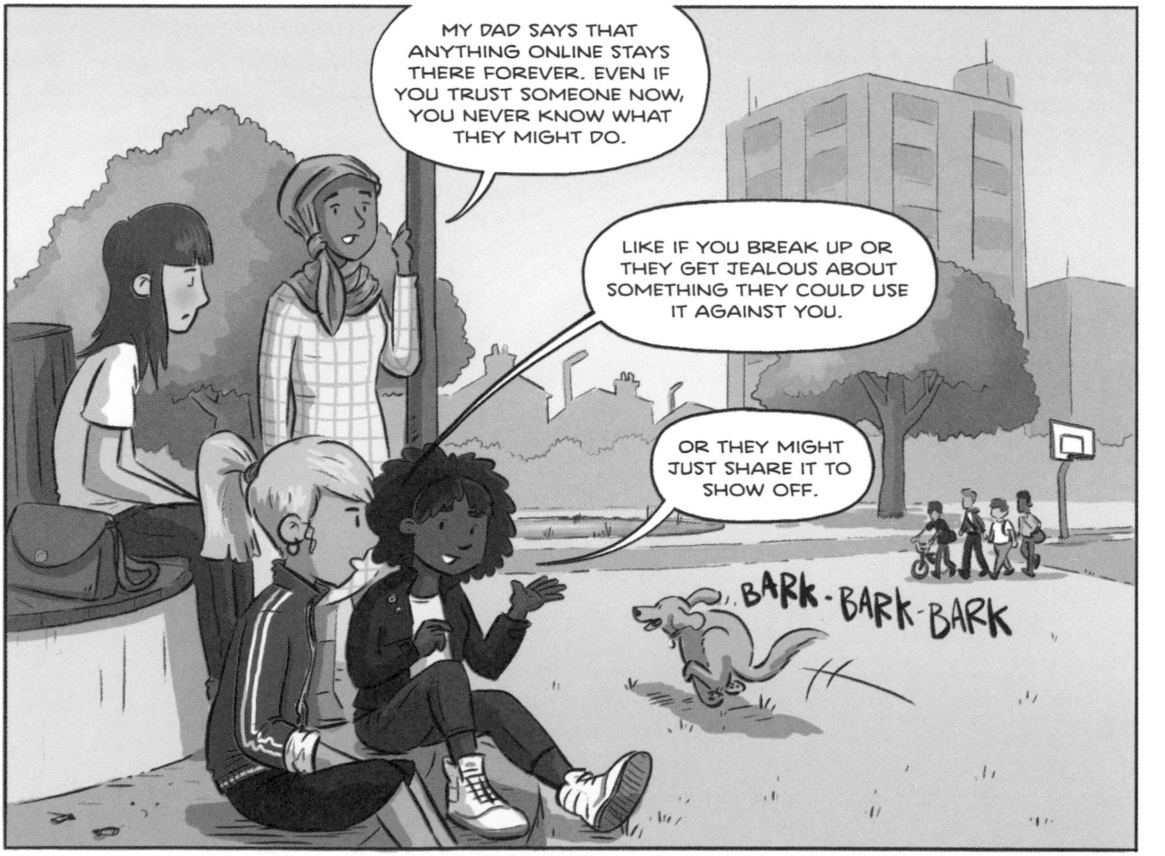
MY DAD SAYS THAT ANYTHING ONLINE STAYS THERE FOREVER. EVEN IF YOU TRUST SOMEONE NOW, YOU NEVER KNOW WHAT THEY MIGHT DO.
LIKE IF YOU BREAK UP OR THEY GET JEALOUS ABOUT SOMETHING THEY COULD USE IT AGAINST YOU.
OR THEY MIGHT JUST SHARE IT TO SHOW OFF.
BARK-BARK-BARK

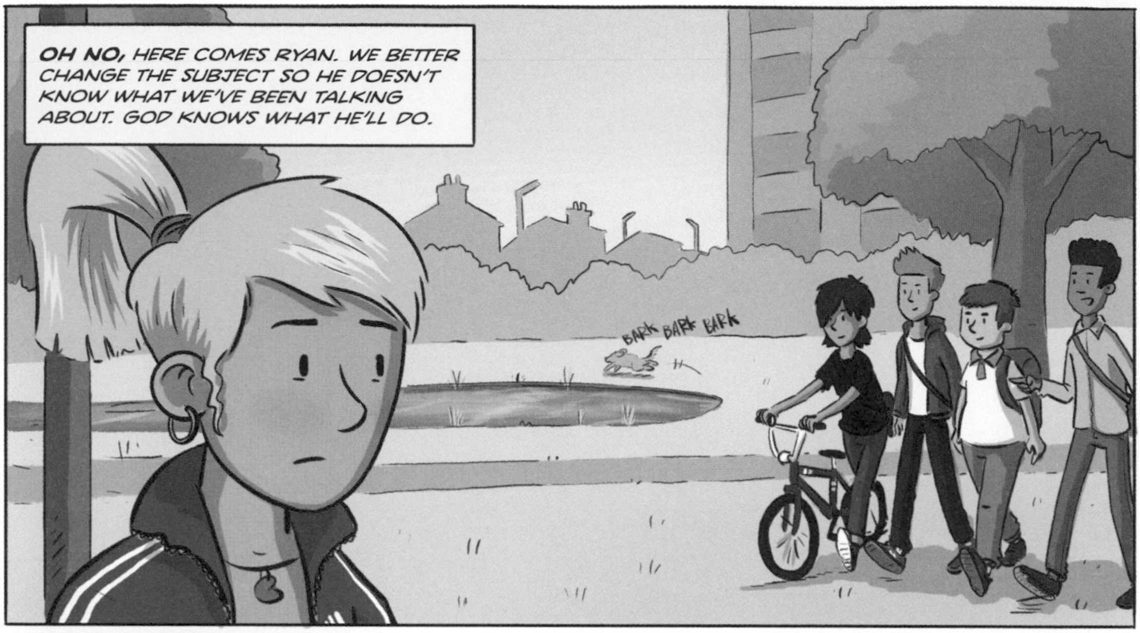
OH NO, HERE COMES RYAN. WE BETTER CHANGE THE SUBJECT SO HE DOESN'T KNOW WHAT WE'VE BEEN TALKING ABOUT. GOD KNOWS WHAT HE'LL DO.
BARK BARK BARK

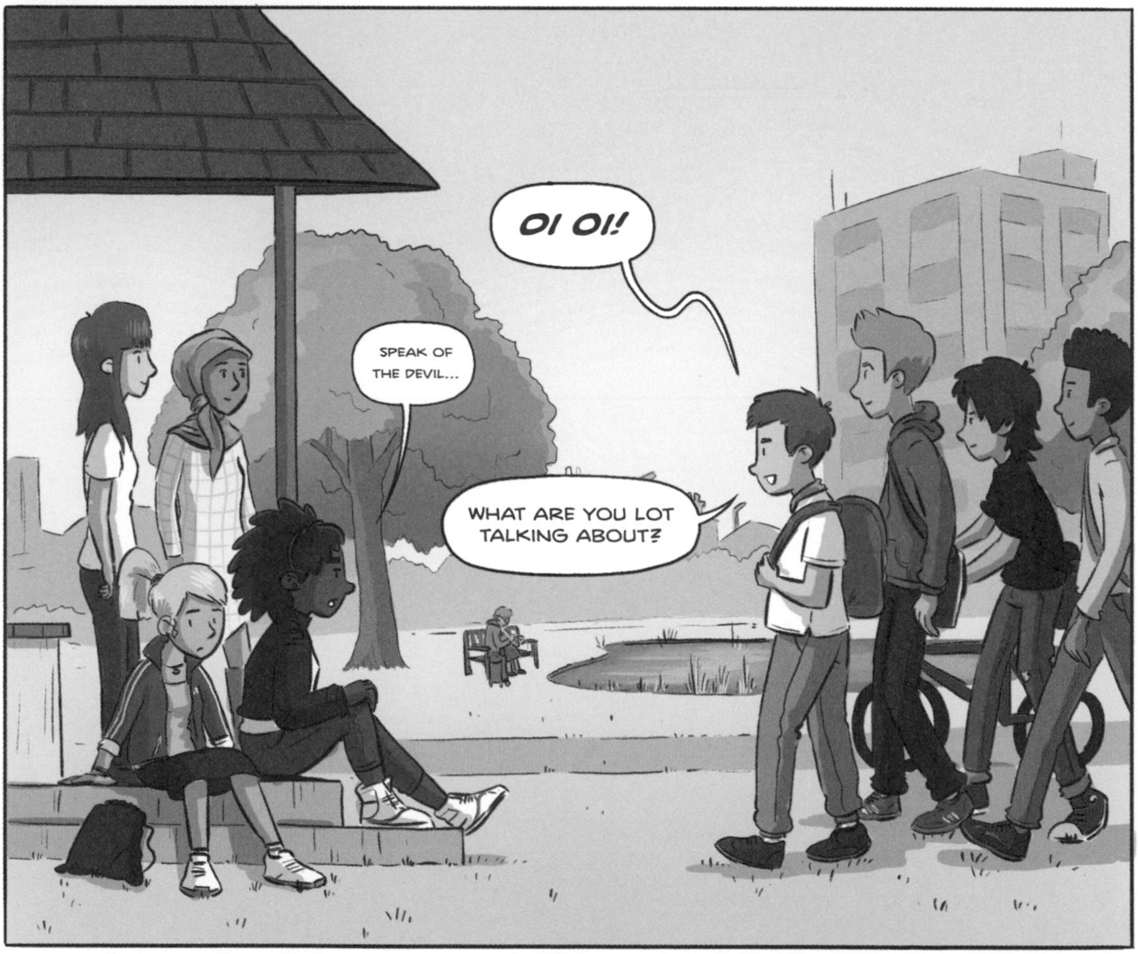
OI OI!
SPEAK OF THE DEVIL...
WHAT ARE YOU LOT TALKING ABOUT?

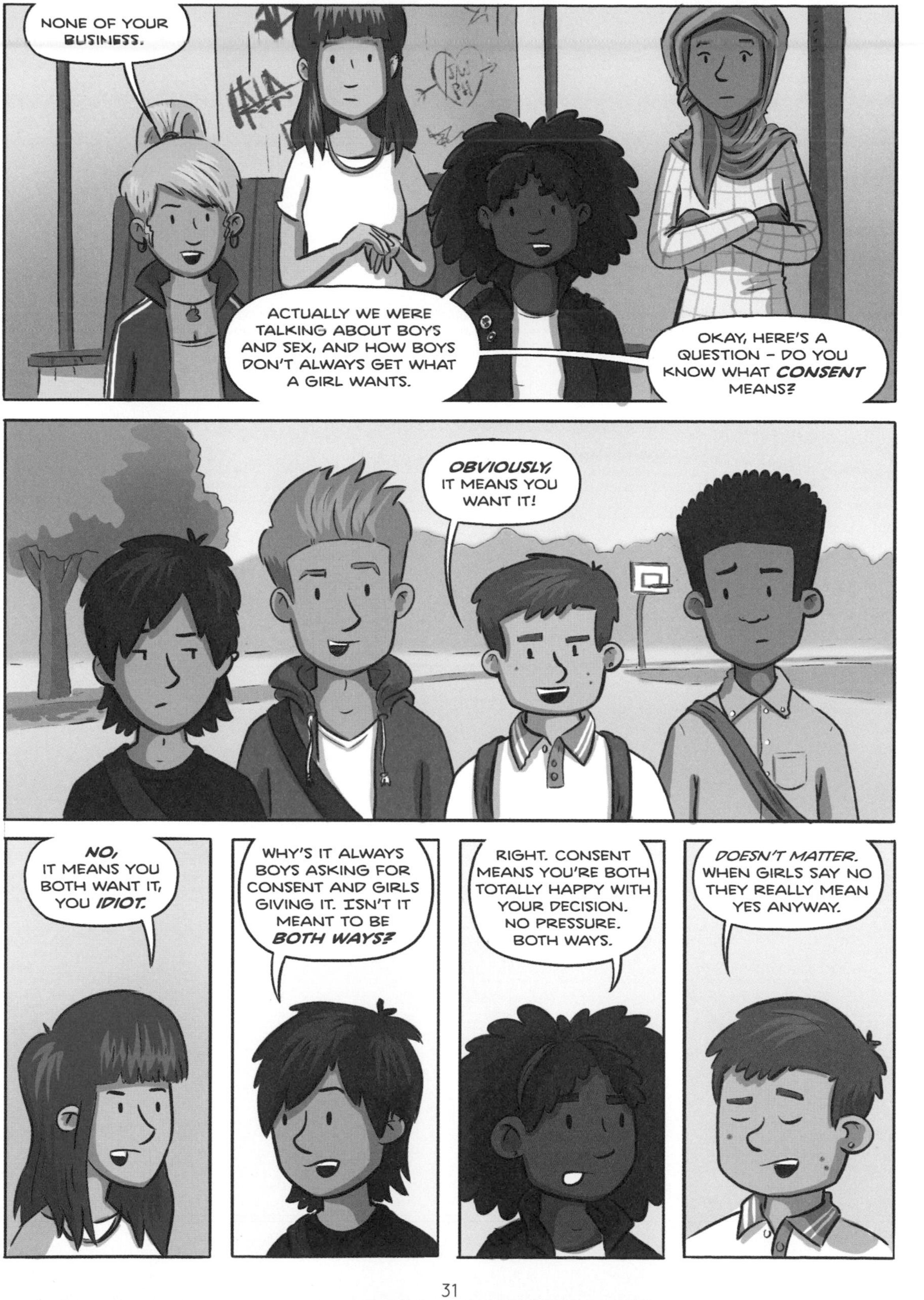
NONE OF YOUR BUSINESS.
ACTUALLY WE WERE TALKING ABOUT BOYS AND SEX, AND HOW BOYS DON'T ALWAYS GET WHAT A GIRL WANTS.
OKAY, HERE'S A QUESTION - DO YOU KNOW WHAT *CONSENT* MEANS?
OBVIOUSLY, IT MEANS YOU WANT IT!
NO, IT MEANS YOU BOTH WANT IT, YOU *IDIOT.*
WHY'S IT ALWAYS BOYS ASKING FOR CONSENT AND GIRLS GIVING IT. ISN'T IT MEANT TO BE *BOTH WAYS?*
RIGHT. CONSENT MEANS YOU'RE BOTH TOTALLY HAPPY WITH YOUR DECISION. NO PRESSURE. BOTH WAYS.
DOESN'T MATTER. WHEN GIRLS SAY NO THEY REALLY MEAN YES ANYWAY.

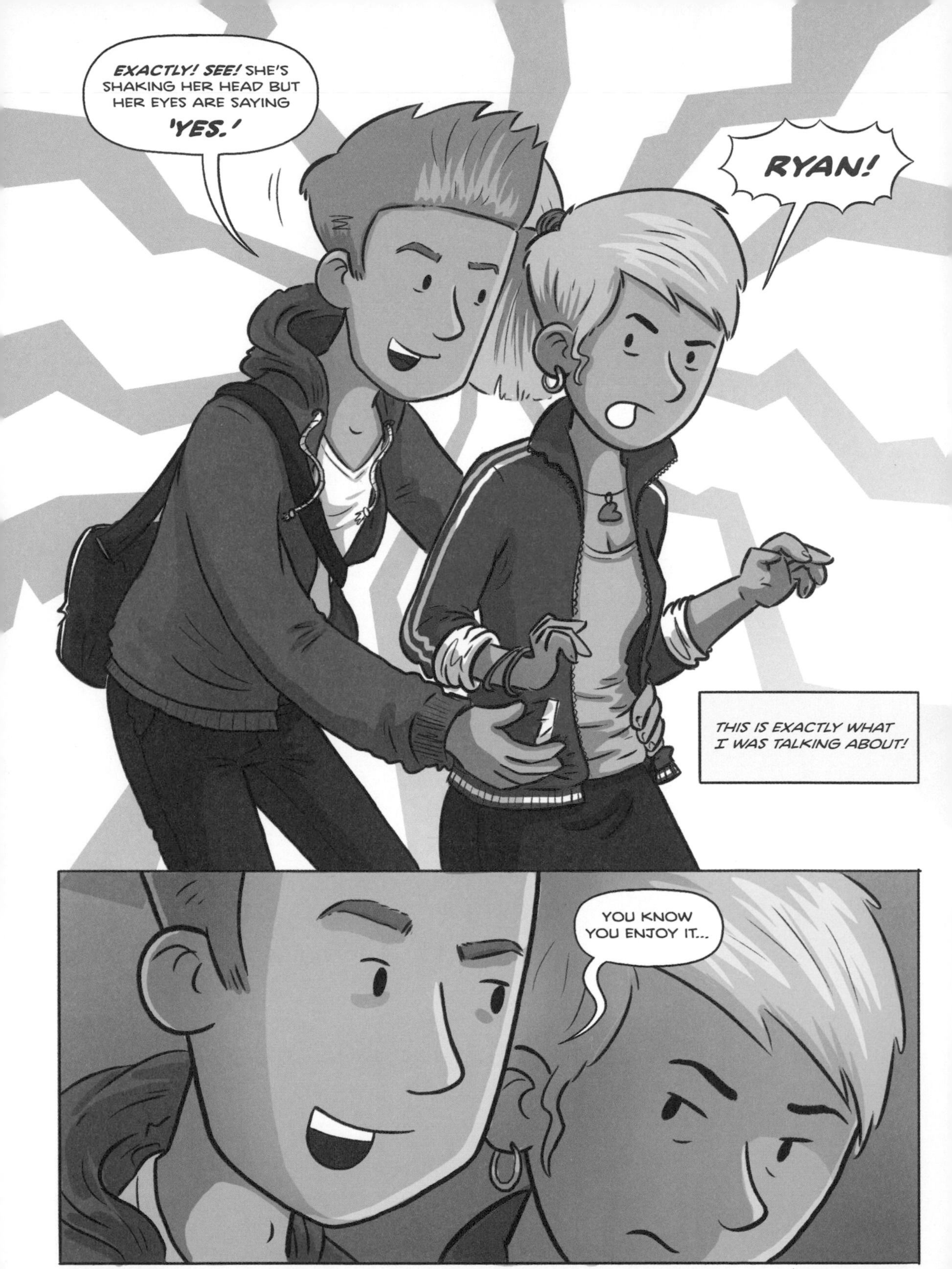
EXACTLY! SEE! SHE'S SHAKING HER HEAD BUT HER EYES ARE SAYING 'YES.'
RYAN!
THIS IS EXACTLY WHAT I WAS TALKING ABOUT!
YOU KNOW YOU ENJOY IT...

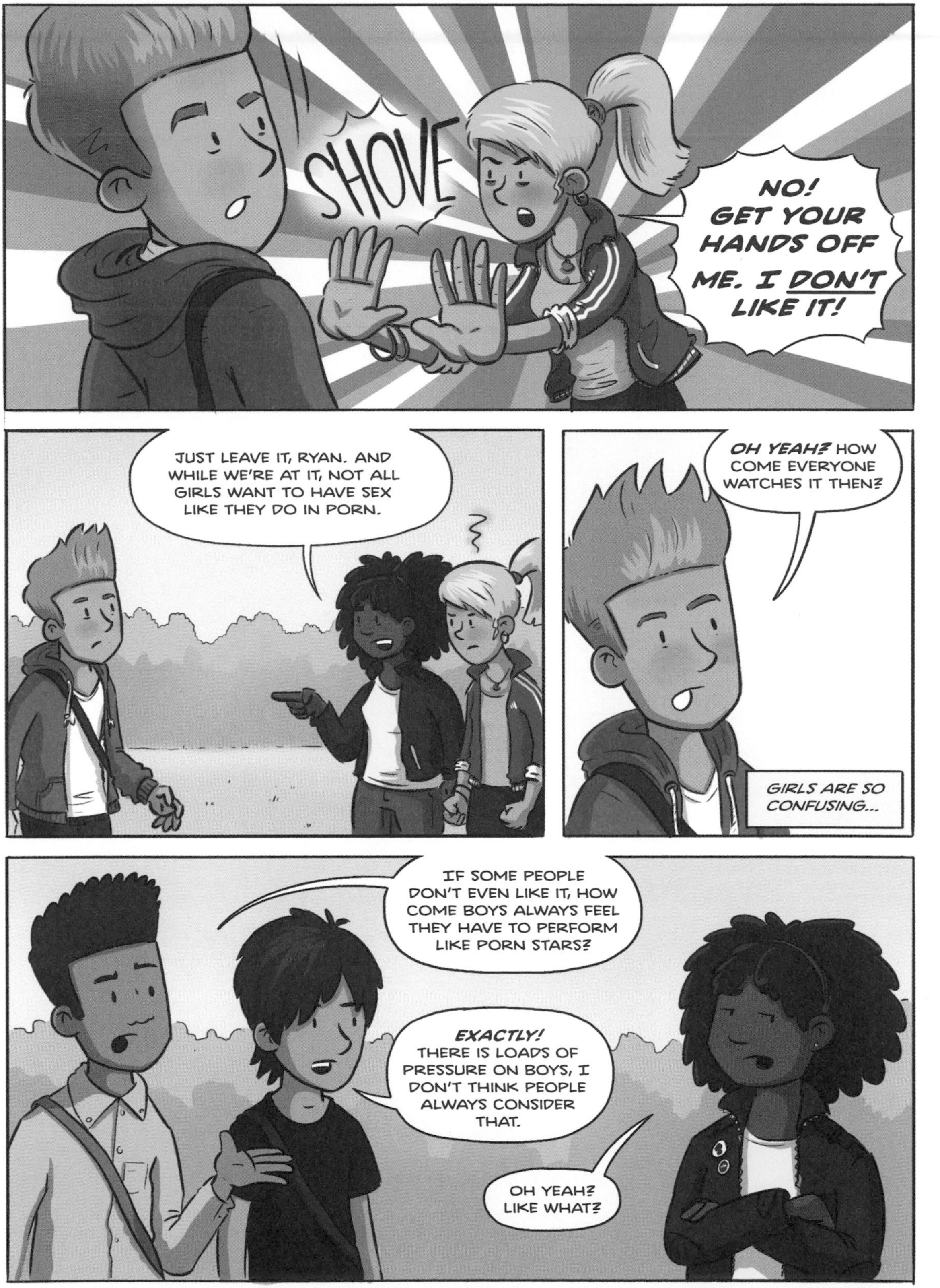
SHOVE
NO! GET YOUR HANDS OFF ME. I DON'T LIKE IT!
JUST LEAVE IT, RYAN. AND WHILE WE'RE AT IT, NOT ALL GIRLS WANT TO HAVE SEX LIKE THEY DO IN PORN.
OH YEAH? HOW COME EVERYONE WATCHES IT THEN?
GIRLS ARE SO CONFUSING...
IF SOME PEOPLE DON'T EVEN LIKE IT, HOW COME BOYS ALWAYS FEEL THEY HAVE TO PERFORM LIKE PORN STARS?
EXACTLY! THERE IS LOADS OF PRESSURE ON BOYS, I DON'T THINK PEOPLE ALWAYS CONSIDER THAT.
OH YEAH? LIKE WHAT?

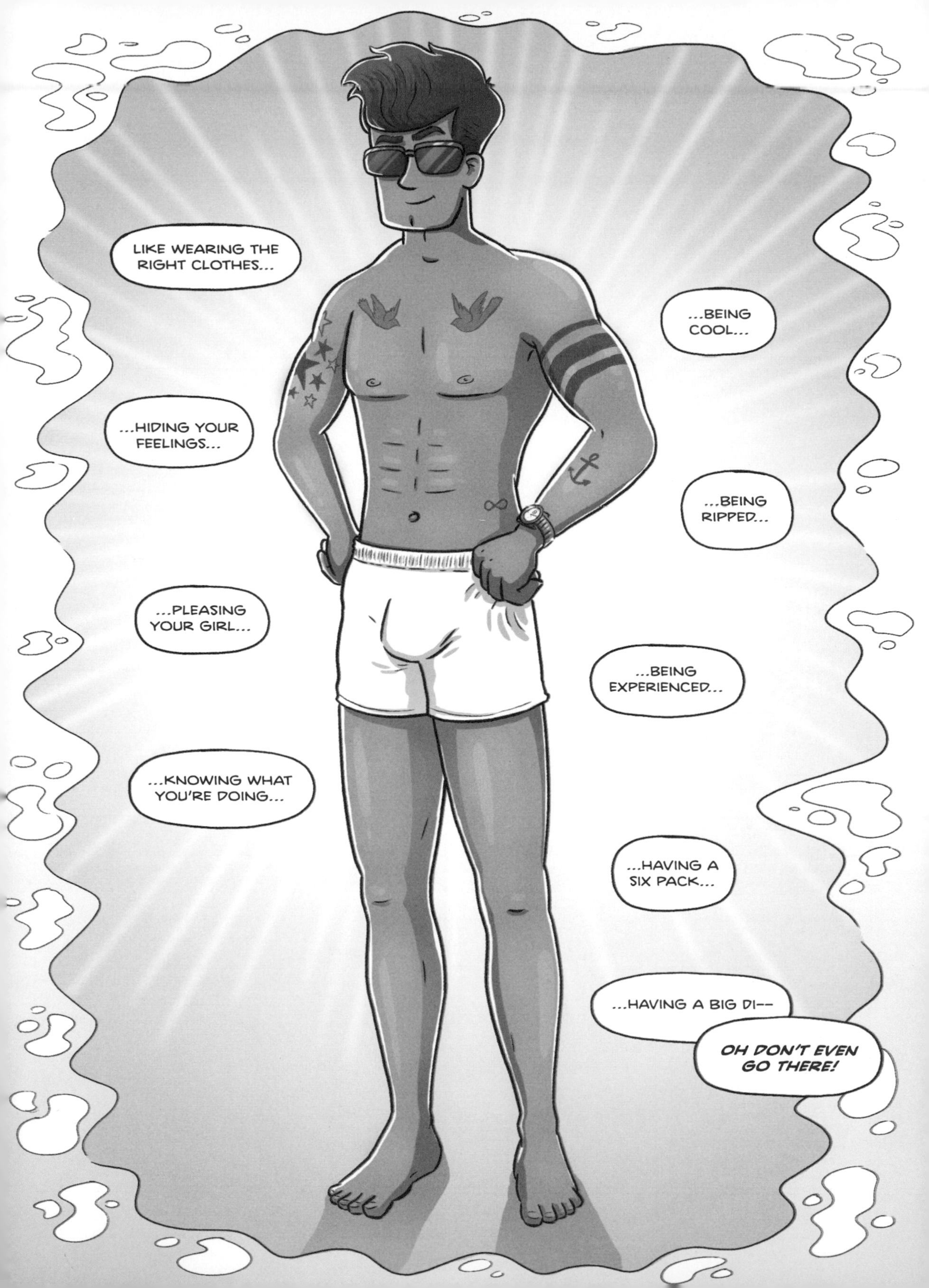
LIKE WEARING THE RIGHT CLOTHES...
...BEING COOL...
...HIDING YOUR FEELINGS...
...BEING RIPPED...
...PLEASING YOUR GIRL...
...BEING EXPERIENCED...
...KNOWING WHAT YOU'RE DOING...
...HAVING A SIX PACK...
...HAVING A BIG DI--
OH DON'T EVEN GO THERE!

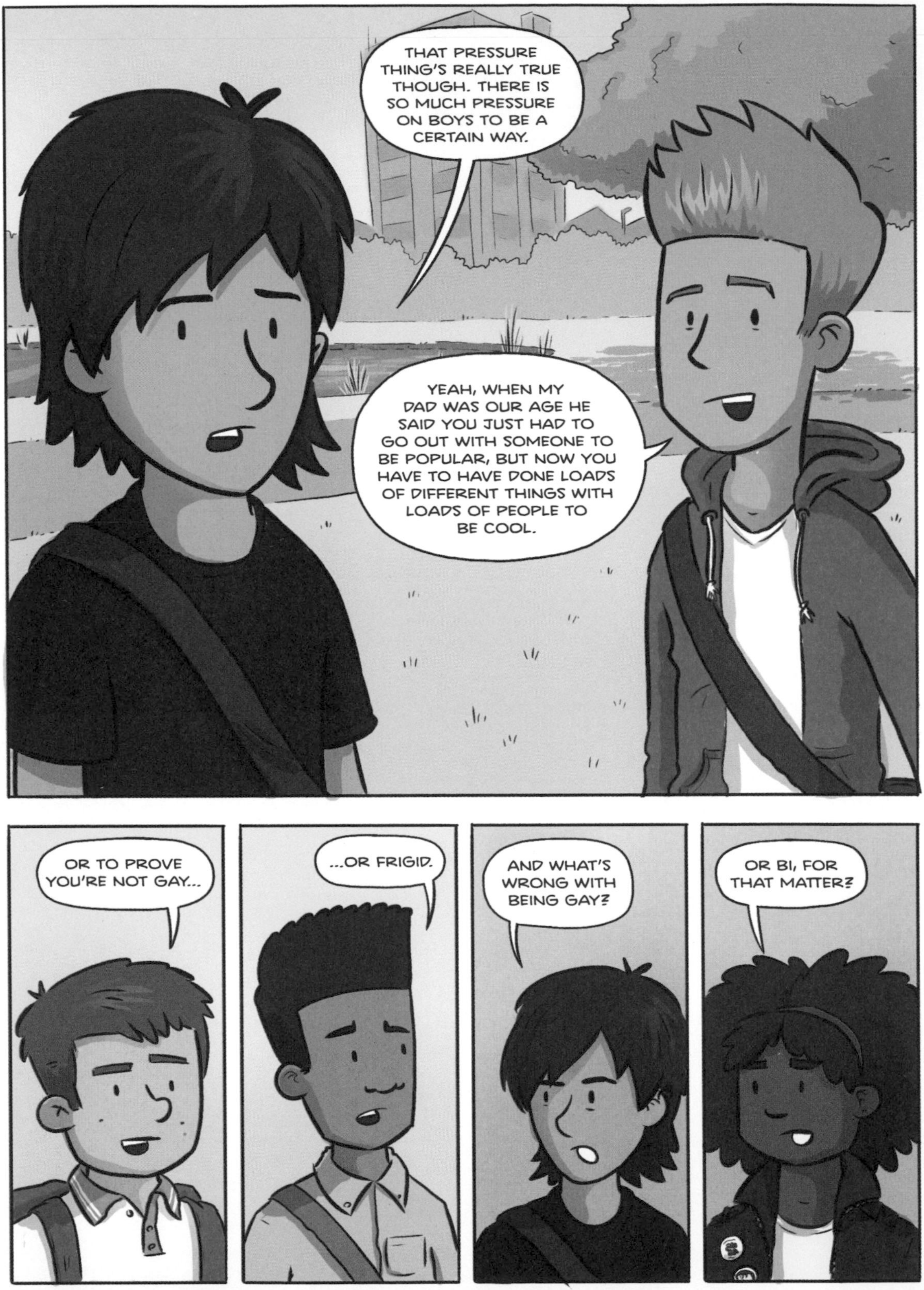
THAT PRESSURE THING'S REALLY TRUE THOUGH. THERE IS SO MUCH PRESSURE ON BOYS TO BE A CERTAIN WAY.
YEAH, WHEN MY DAD WAS OUR AGE HE SAID YOU JUST HAD TO GO OUT WITH SOMEONE TO BE POPULAR, BUT NOW YOU HAVE TO HAVE DONE LOADS OF DIFFERENT THINGS WITH LOADS OF PEOPLE TO BE COOL.
OR TO PROVE YOU'RE NOT GAY...
...OR FRIGID.
AND WHAT'S WRONG WITH BEING GAY?
OR BI, FOR THAT MATTER?

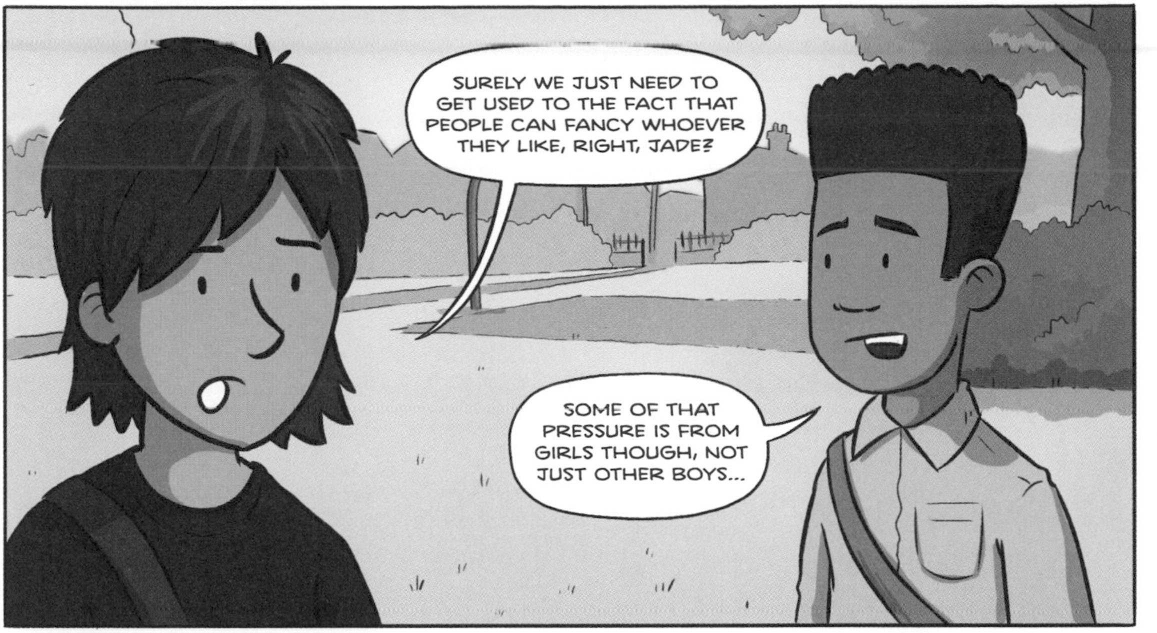
SURELY WE JUST NEED TO GET USED TO THE FACT THAT PEOPLE CAN FANCY WHOEVER THEY LIKE, RIGHT, JADE?
SOME OF THAT PRESSURE IS FROM GIRLS THOUGH, NOT JUST OTHER BOYS...

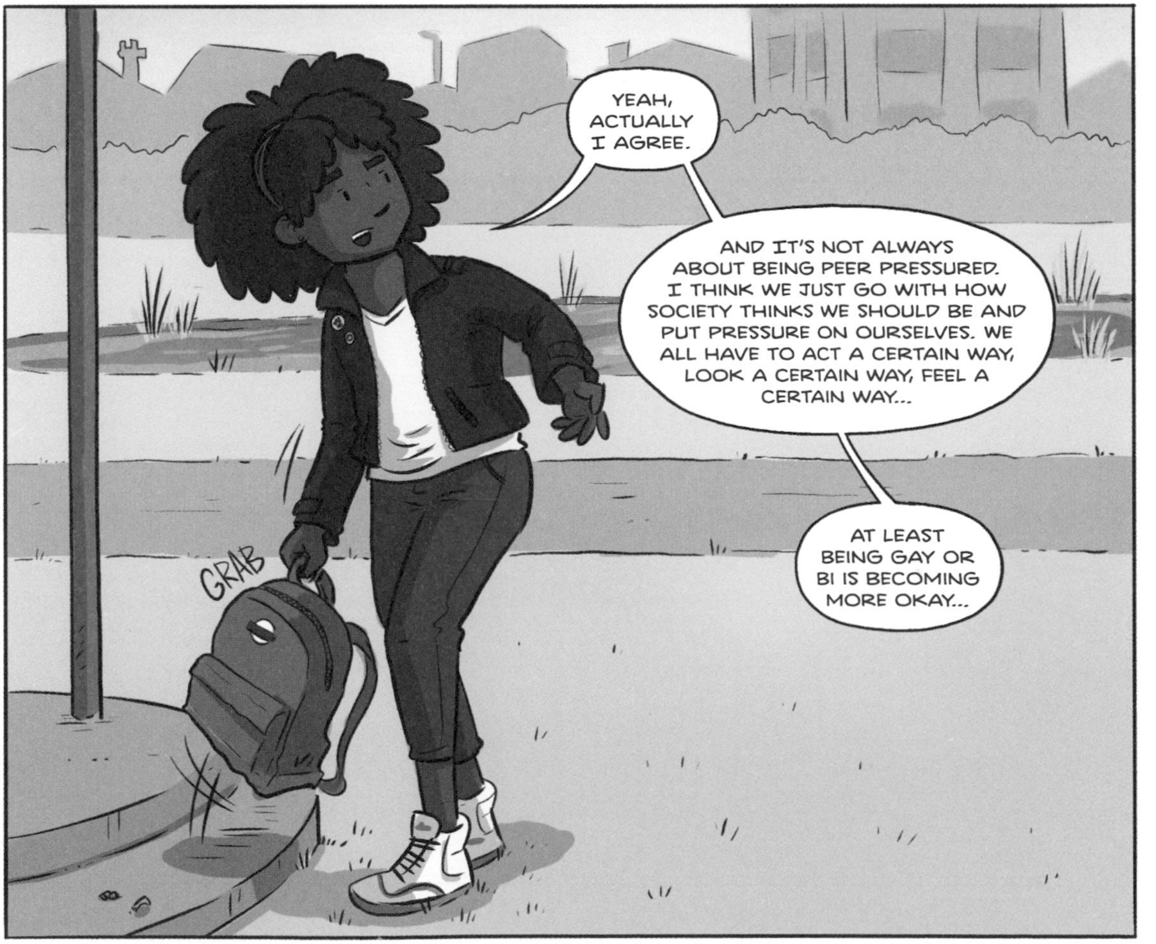
YEAH, ACTUALLY I AGREE.
AND IT'S NOT ALWAYS ABOUT BEING PEER PRESSURED. I THINK WE JUST GO WITH HOW SOCIETY THINKS WE SHOULD BE AND PUT PRESSURE ON OURSELVES. WE ALL HAVE TO ACT A CERTAIN WAY, LOOK A CERTAIN WAY, FEEL A CERTAIN WAY...
AT LEAST BEING GAY OR BI IS BECOMING MORE OKAY...
GRAB

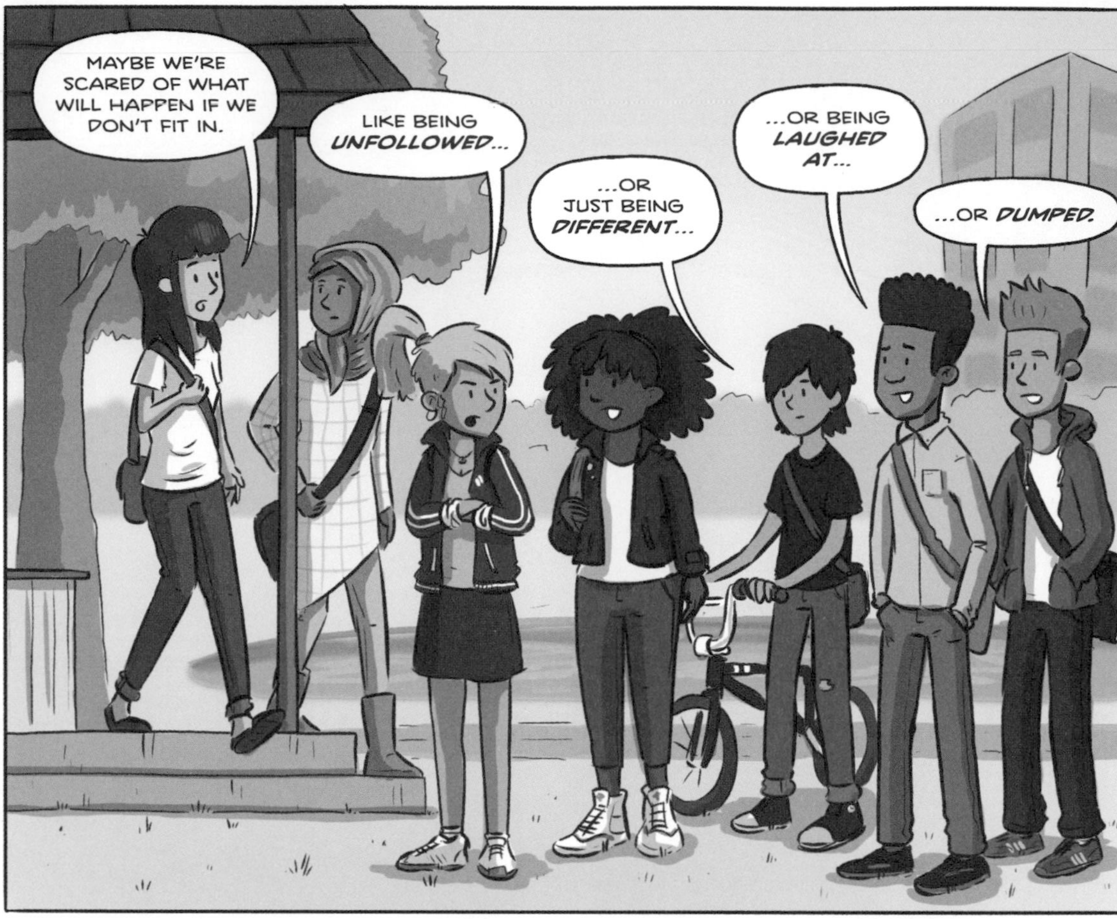
MAYBE WE'RE SCARED OF WHAT WILL HAPPEN IF WE DON'T FIT IN.
LIKE BEING UNFOLLOWED...
...OR JUST BEING DIFFERENT...
...OR BEING LAUGHED AT...
...OR DUMPED.

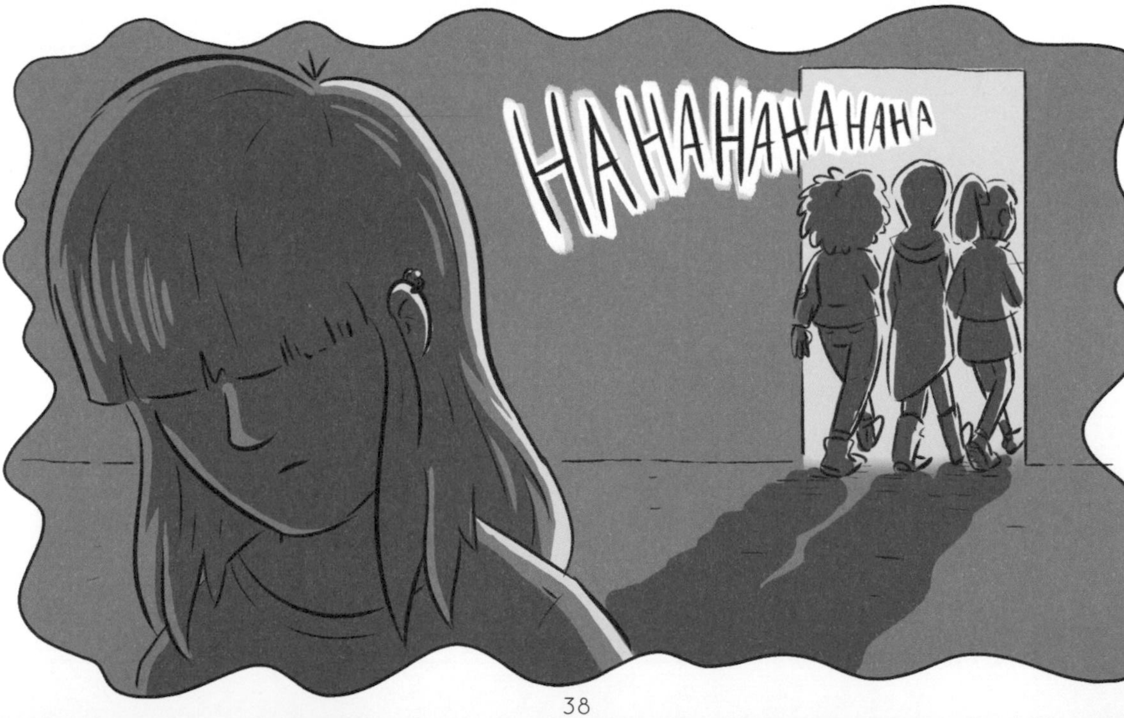
HAHAHAHAHAHAHA

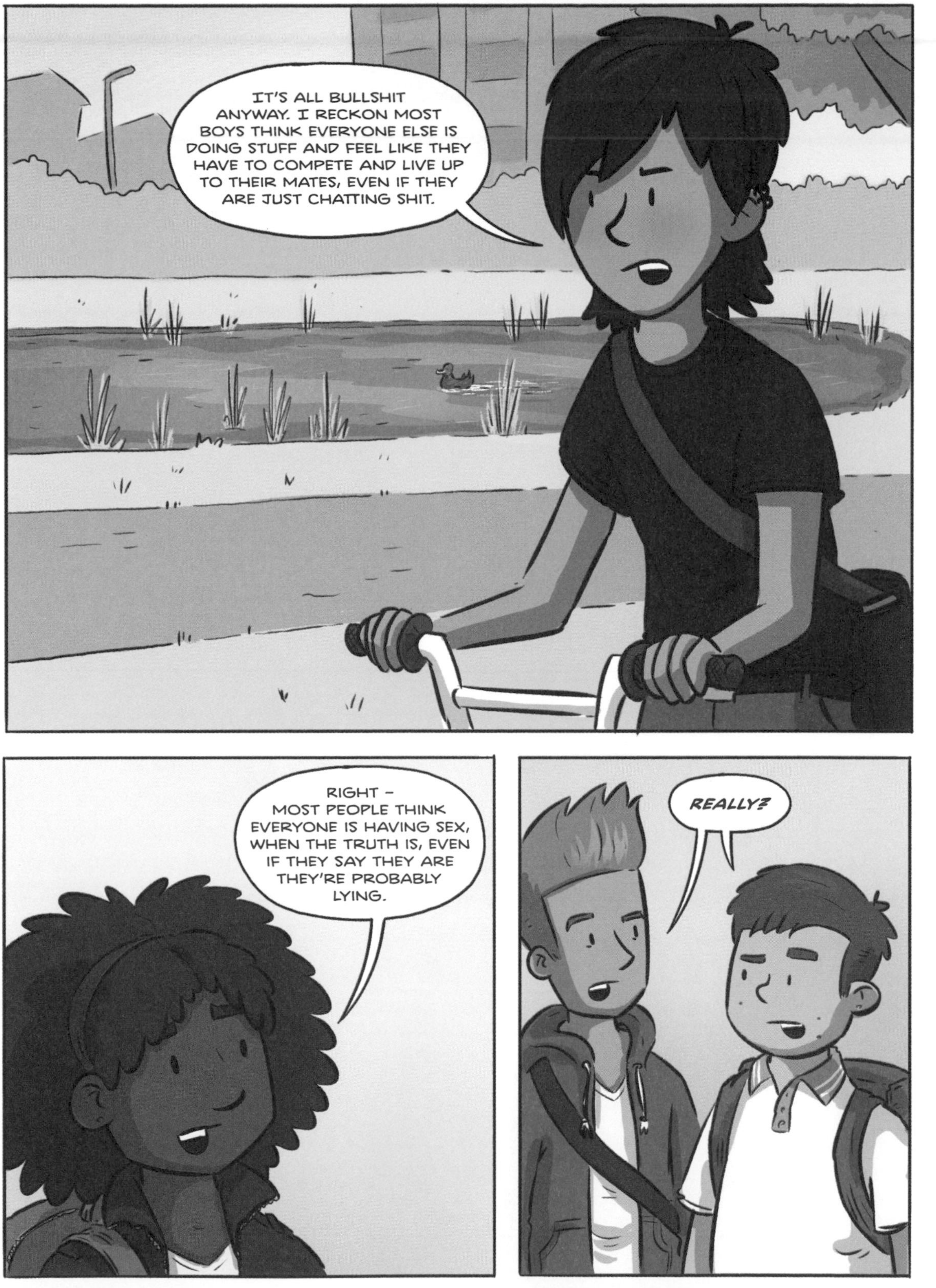
IT'S ALL BULLSHIT ANYWAY. I RECKON MOST BOYS THINK EVERYONE ELSE IS DOING STUFF AND FEEL LIKE THEY HAVE TO COMPETE AND LIVE UP TO THEIR MATES, EVEN IF THEY ARE JUST CHATTING SHIT.
RIGHT – MOST PEOPLE THINK EVERYONE IS HAVING SEX, WHEN THE TRUTH IS, EVEN IF THEY SAY THEY ARE THEY'RE PROBABLY LYING.
REALLY?

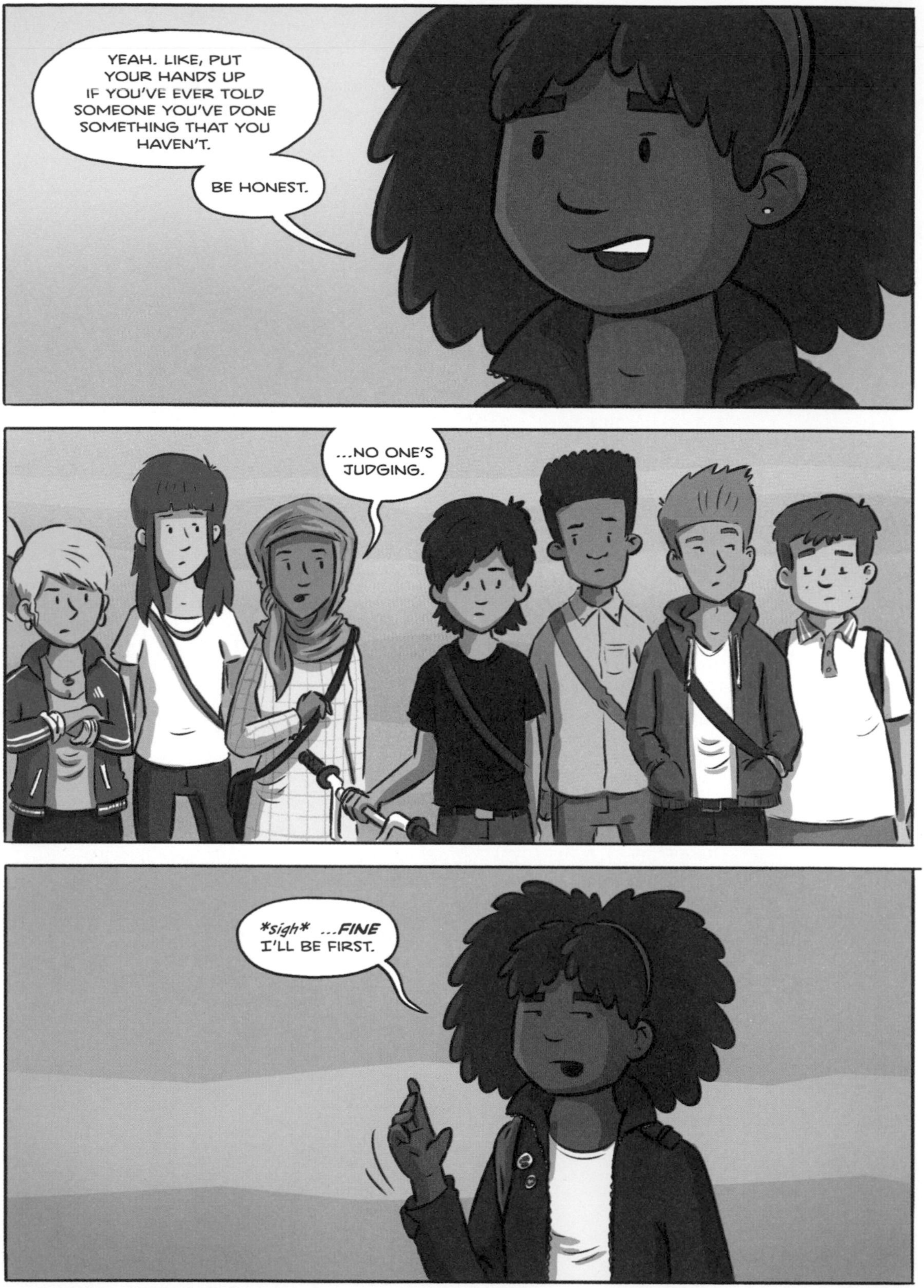
YEAH. LIKE, PUT YOUR HANDS UP IF YOU'VE EVER TOLD SOMEONE YOU'VE DONE SOMETHING THAT YOU HAVEN'T.
BE HONEST.
...NO ONE'S JUDGING.
sigh ...FINE I'LL BE FIRST.

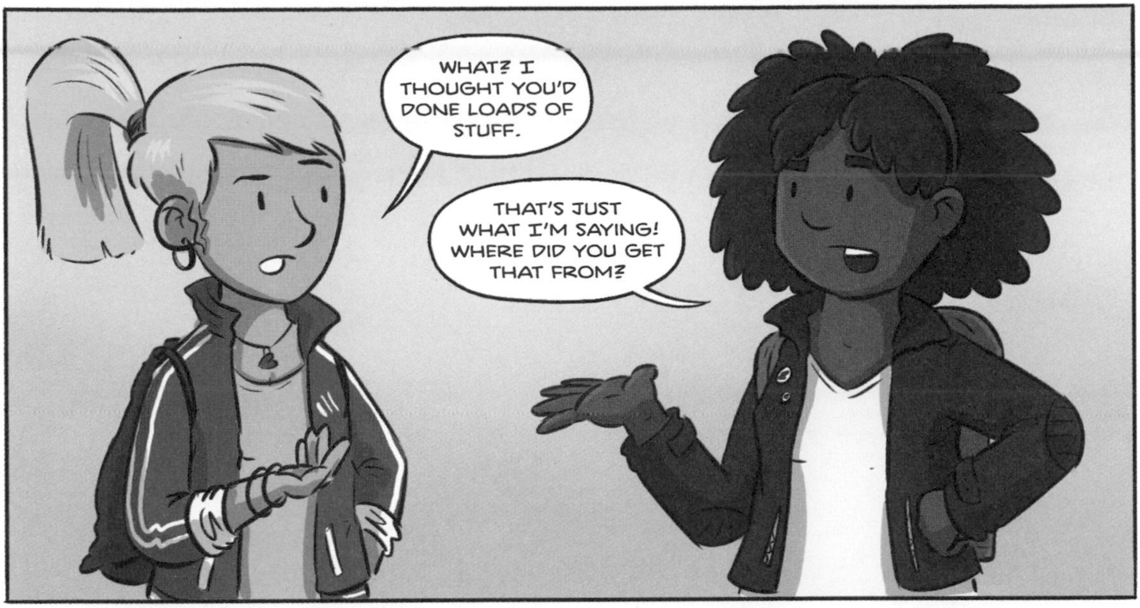
WHAT? I THOUGHT YOU'D DONE LOADS OF STUFF.
THAT'S JUST WHAT I'M SAYING! WHERE DID YOU GET THAT FROM?

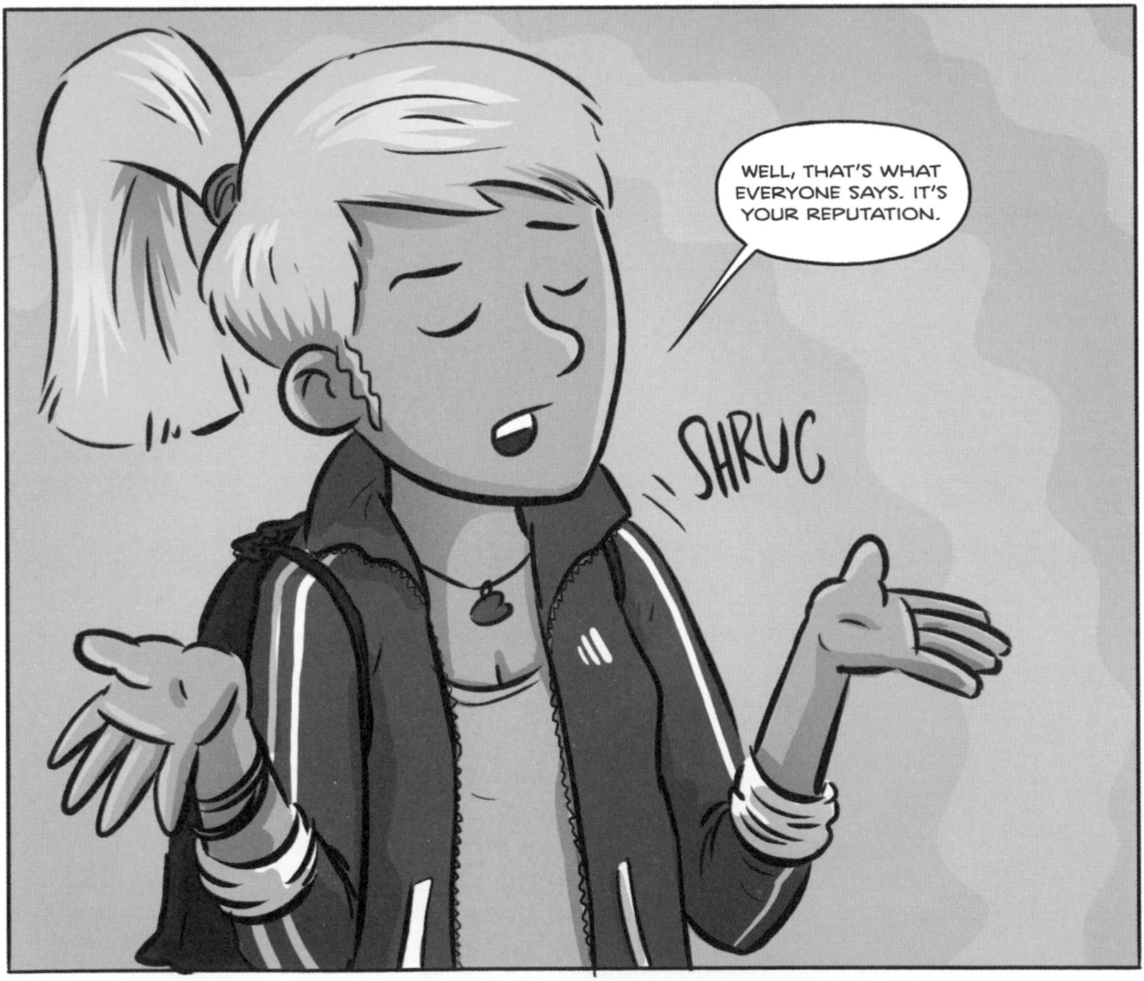
WELL, THAT'S WHAT EVERYONE SAYS. IT'S YOUR REPUTATION.
SHRUG

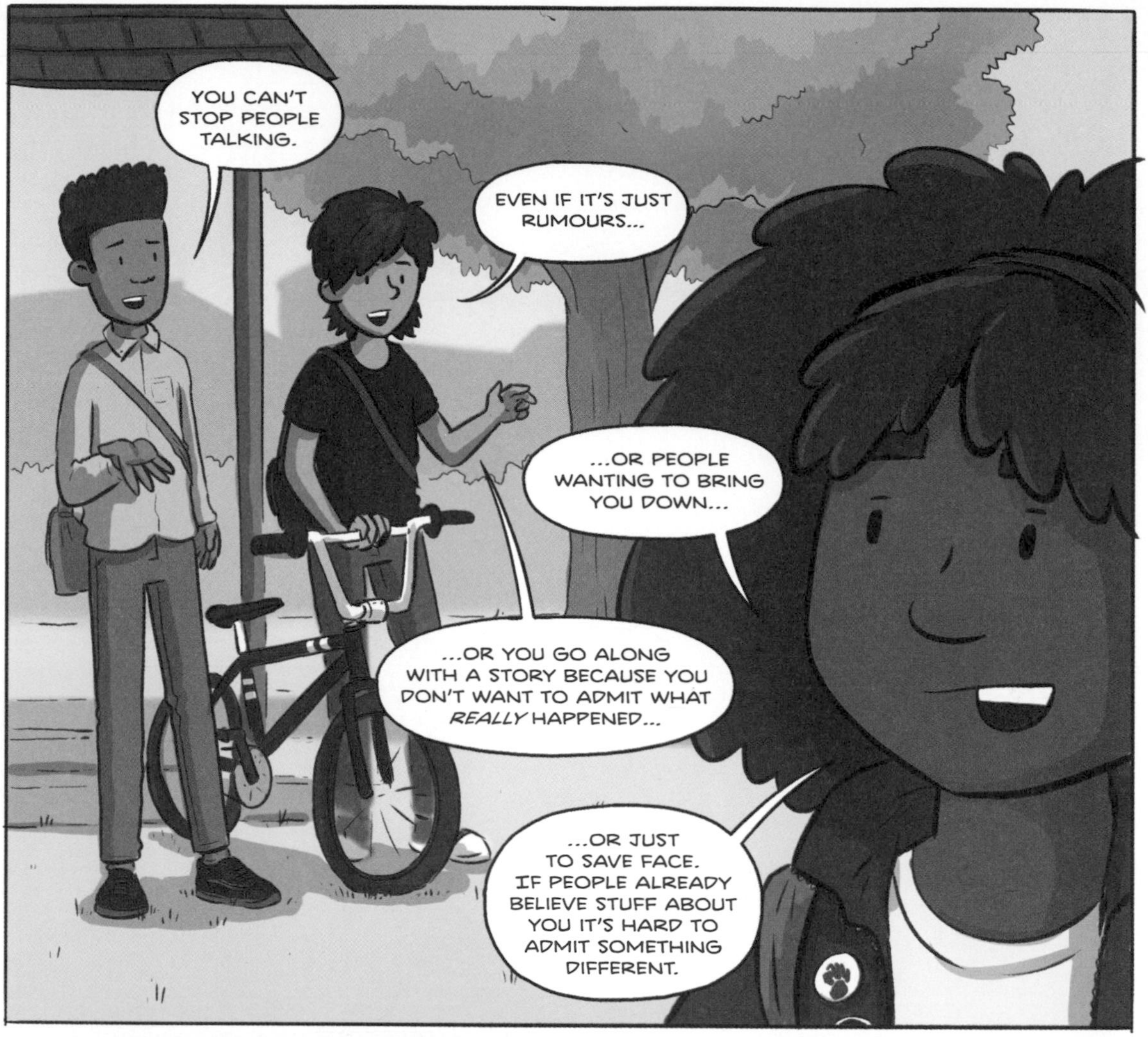
YOU CAN'T STOP PEOPLE TALKING.
EVEN IF IT'S JUST RUMOURS...
...OR PEOPLE WANTING TO BRING YOU DOWN...
...OR YOU GO ALONG WITH A STORY BECAUSE YOU DON'T WANT TO ADMIT WHAT *REALLY* HAPPENED...
...OR JUST TO SAVE FACE. IF PEOPLE ALREADY BELIEVE STUFF ABOUT YOU IT'S HARD TO ADMIT SOMETHING DIFFERENT.

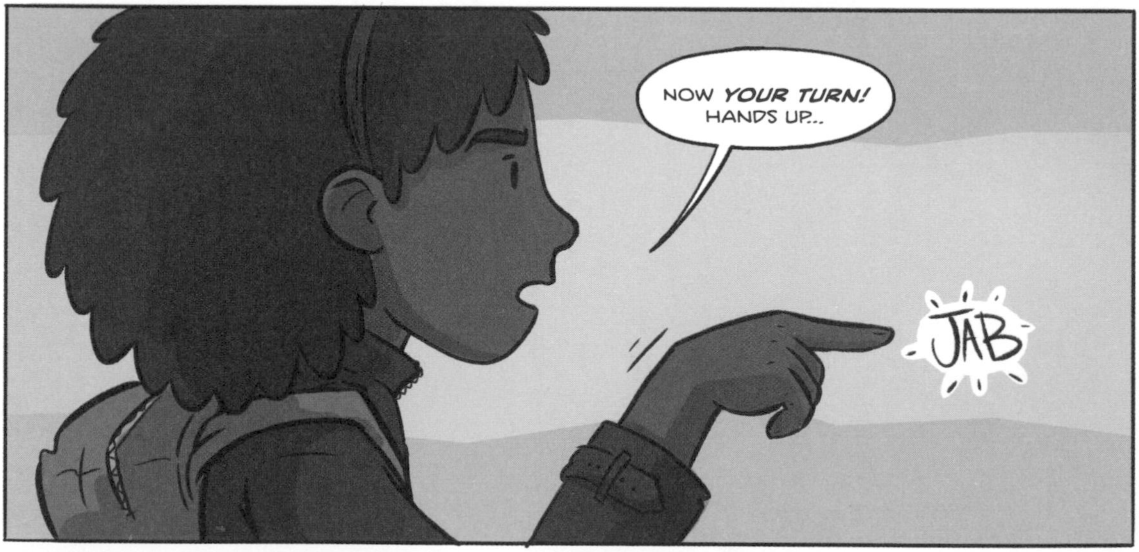
NOW ***YOUR TURN!*** HANDS UP...
JAB

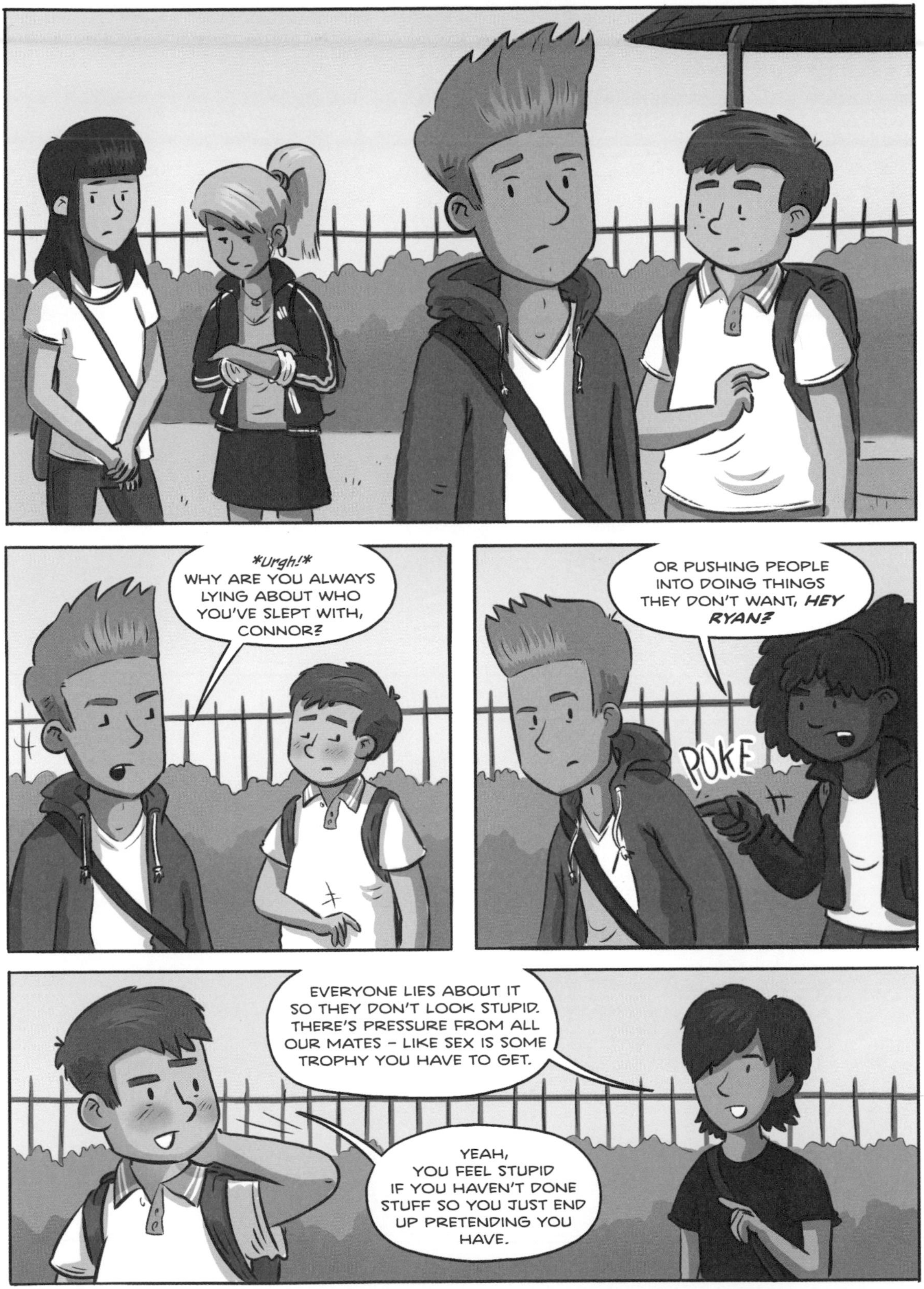
Urgh!
WHY ARE YOU ALWAYS LYING ABOUT WHO YOU'VE SLEPT WITH, CONNOR?
OR PUSHING PEOPLE INTO DOING THINGS THEY DON'T WANT, HEY RYAN?
POKE
EVERYONE LIES ABOUT IT SO THEY DON'T LOOK STUPID. THERE'S PRESSURE FROM ALL OUR MATES – LIKE SEX IS SOME TROPHY YOU HAVE TO GET.
YEAH, YOU FEEL STUPID IF YOU HAVEN'T DONE STUFF SO YOU JUST END UP PRETENDING YOU HAVE.

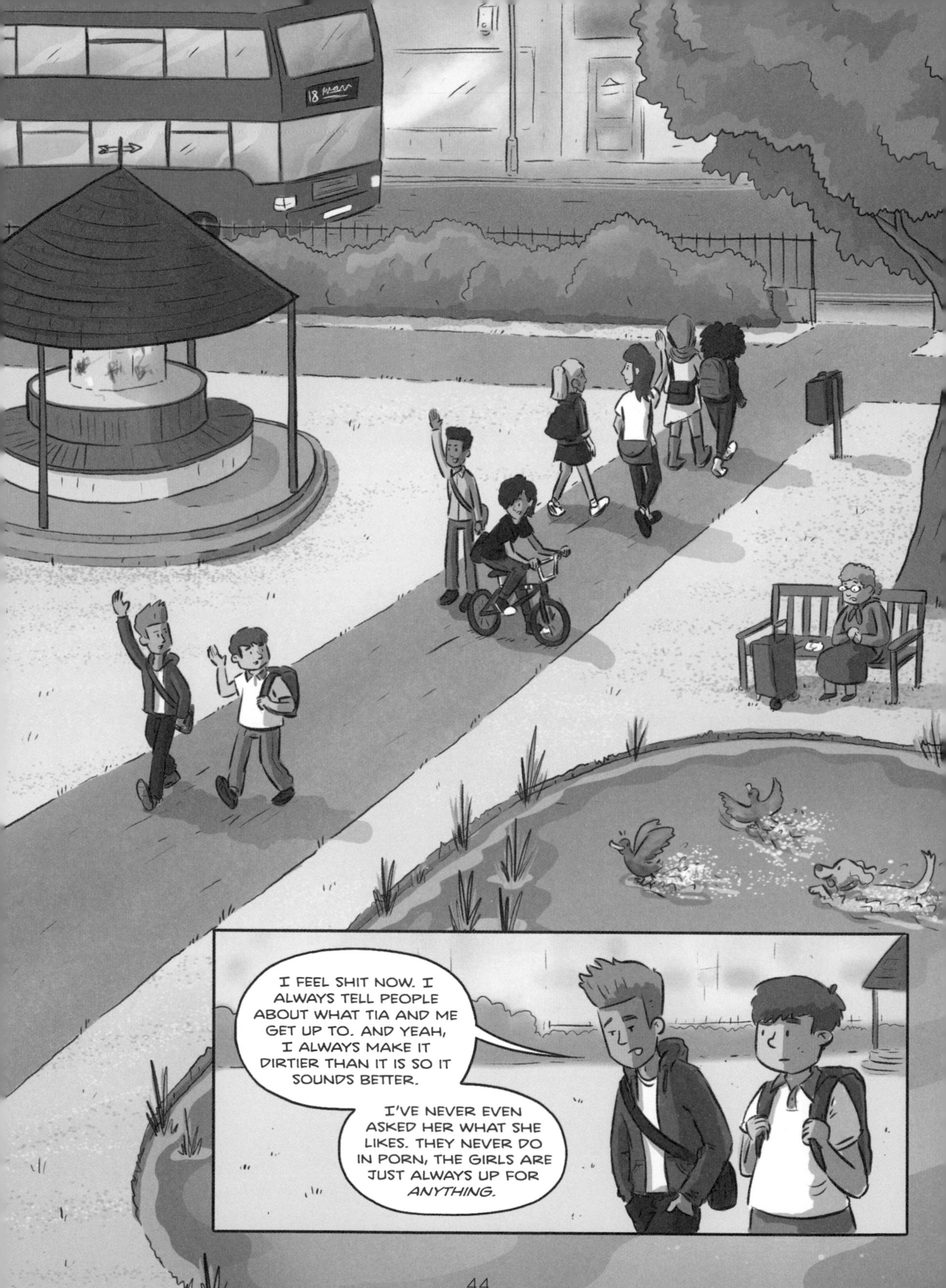
I FEEL SHIT NOW. I ALWAYS TELL PEOPLE ABOUT WHAT TIA AND ME GET UP TO. AND YEAH, I ALWAYS MAKE IT DIRTIER THAN IT IS SO IT SOUNDS BETTER.
I'VE NEVER EVEN ASKED HER WHAT SHE LIKES. THEY NEVER DO IN PORN, THE GIRLS ARE JUST ALWAYS UP FOR *ANYTHING*.

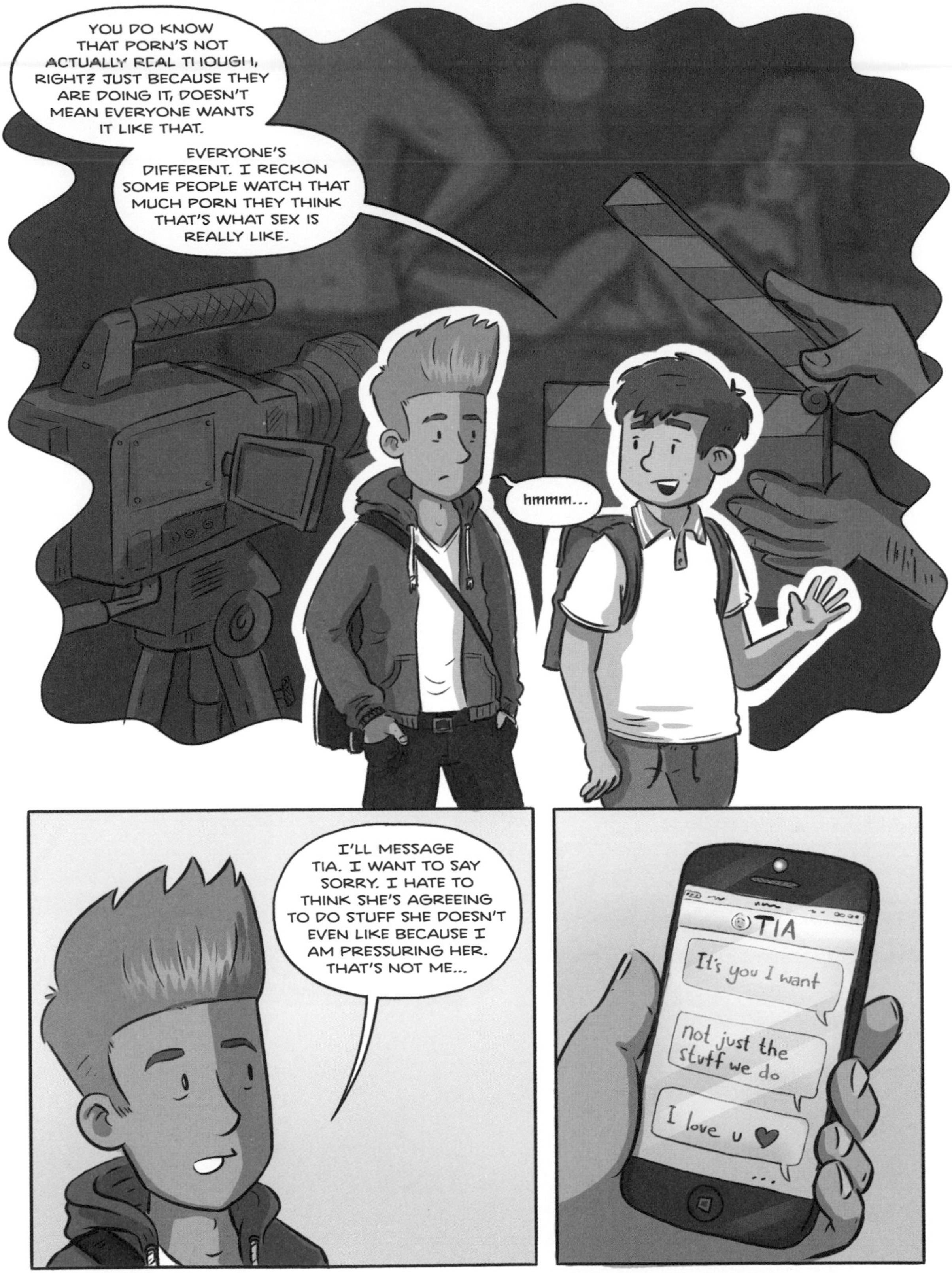
YOU DO KNOW THAT PORN'S NOT ACTUALLY REAL THOUGH, RIGHT? JUST BECAUSE THEY ARE DOING IT, DOESN'T MEAN EVERYONE WANTS IT LIKE THAT.
EVERYONE'S DIFFERENT. I RECKON SOME PEOPLE WATCH THAT MUCH PORN THEY THINK THAT'S WHAT SEX IS REALLY LIKE.
hmmm...
I'LL MESSAGE TIA. I WANT TO SAY SORRY. I HATE TO THINK SHE'S AGREEING TO DO STUFF SHE DOESN'T EVEN LIKE BECAUSE I AM PRESSURING HER. THAT'S NOT ME...
TIA
It's you I want
not just the stuff we do
I love u
...

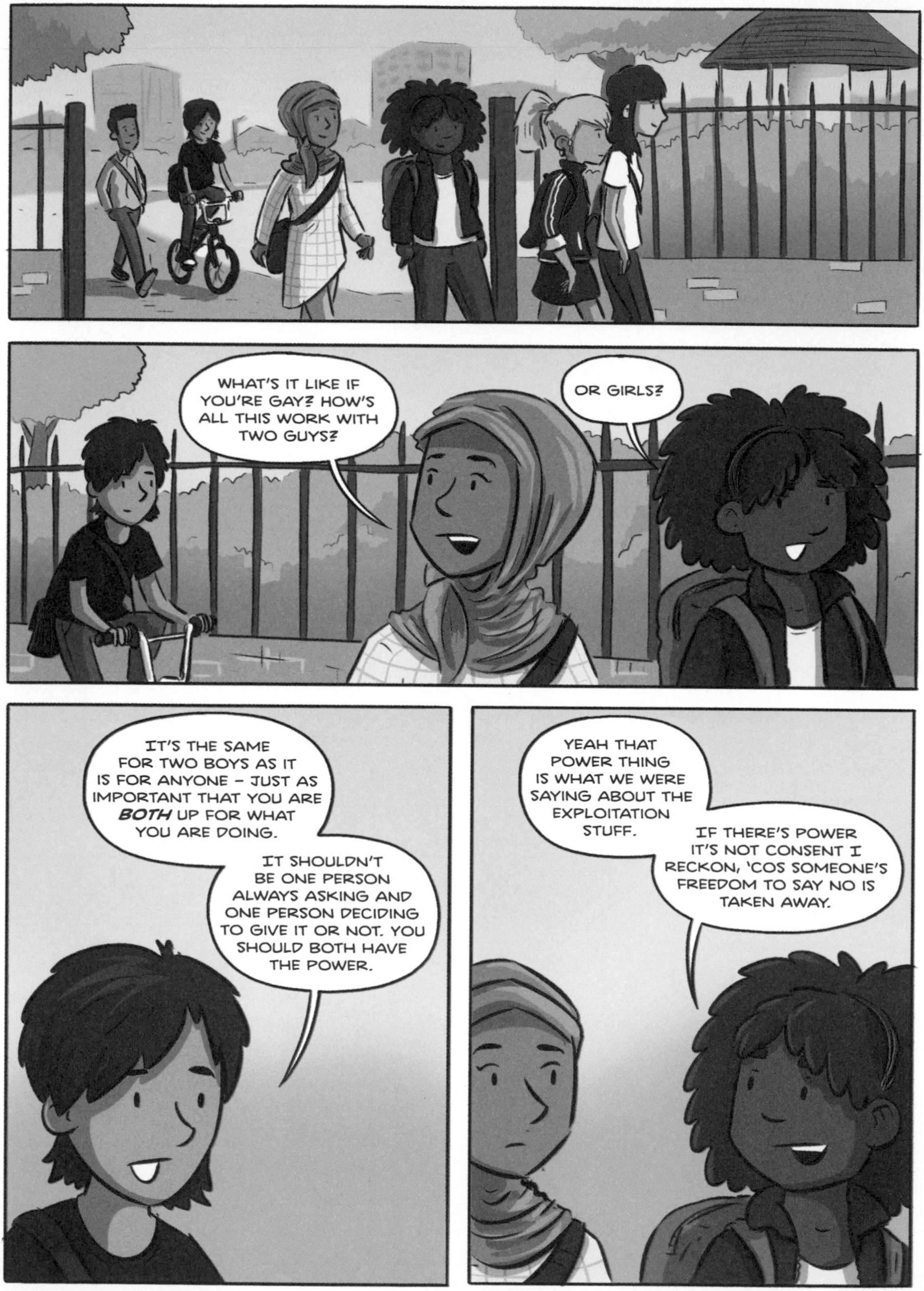
WHAT'S IT LIKE IF YOU'RE GAY? HOW'S ALL THIS WORK WITH TWO GUYS?
OR GIRLS?
IT'S THE SAME FOR TWO BOYS AS IT IS FOR ANYONE – JUST AS IMPORTANT THAT YOU ARE BOTH UP FOR WHAT YOU ARE DOING.
IT SHOULDN'T BE ONE PERSON ALWAYS ASKING AND ONE PERSON DECIDING TO GIVE IT OR NOT. YOU SHOULD BOTH HAVE THE POWER.
YEAH THAT POWER THING IS WHAT WE WERE SAYING ABOUT THE EXPLOITATION STUFF.
IF THERE'S POWER IT'S NOT CONSENT I RECKON, 'COS SOMEONE'S FREEDOM TO SAY NO IS TAKEN AWAY.

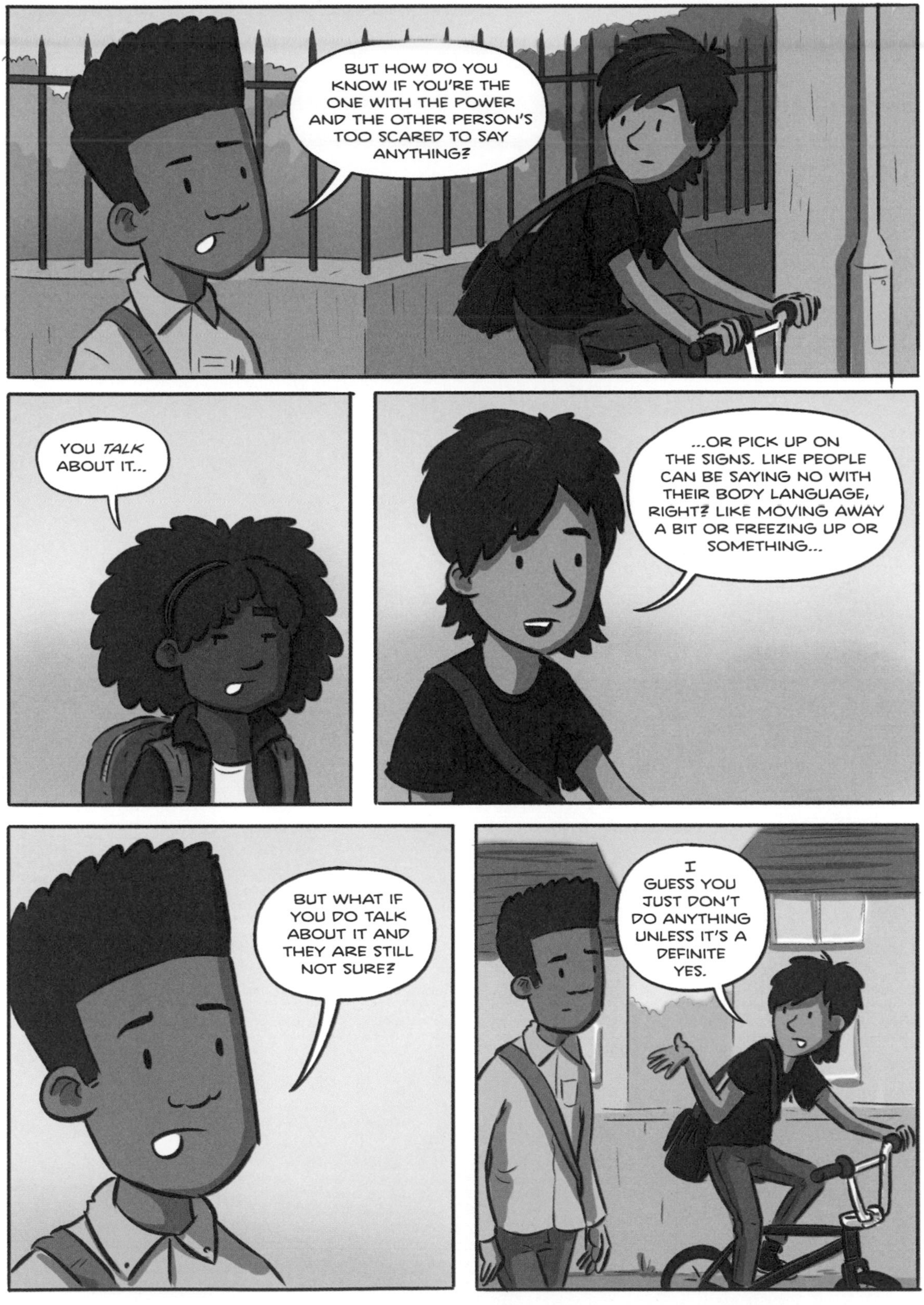
BUT HOW DO YOU KNOW IF YOU'RE THE ONE WITH THE POWER AND THE OTHER PERSON'S TOO SCARED TO SAY ANYTHING?
YOU *TALK* ABOUT IT...
...OR PICK UP ON THE SIGNS. LIKE PEOPLE CAN BE SAYING NO WITH THEIR BODY LANGUAGE, RIGHT? LIKE MOVING AWAY A BIT OR FREEZING UP OR SOMETHING...
BUT WHAT IF YOU DO TALK ABOUT IT AND THEY ARE STILL NOT SURE?
I GUESS YOU JUST DON'T DO ANYTHING UNLESS IT'S A DEFINITE YES.

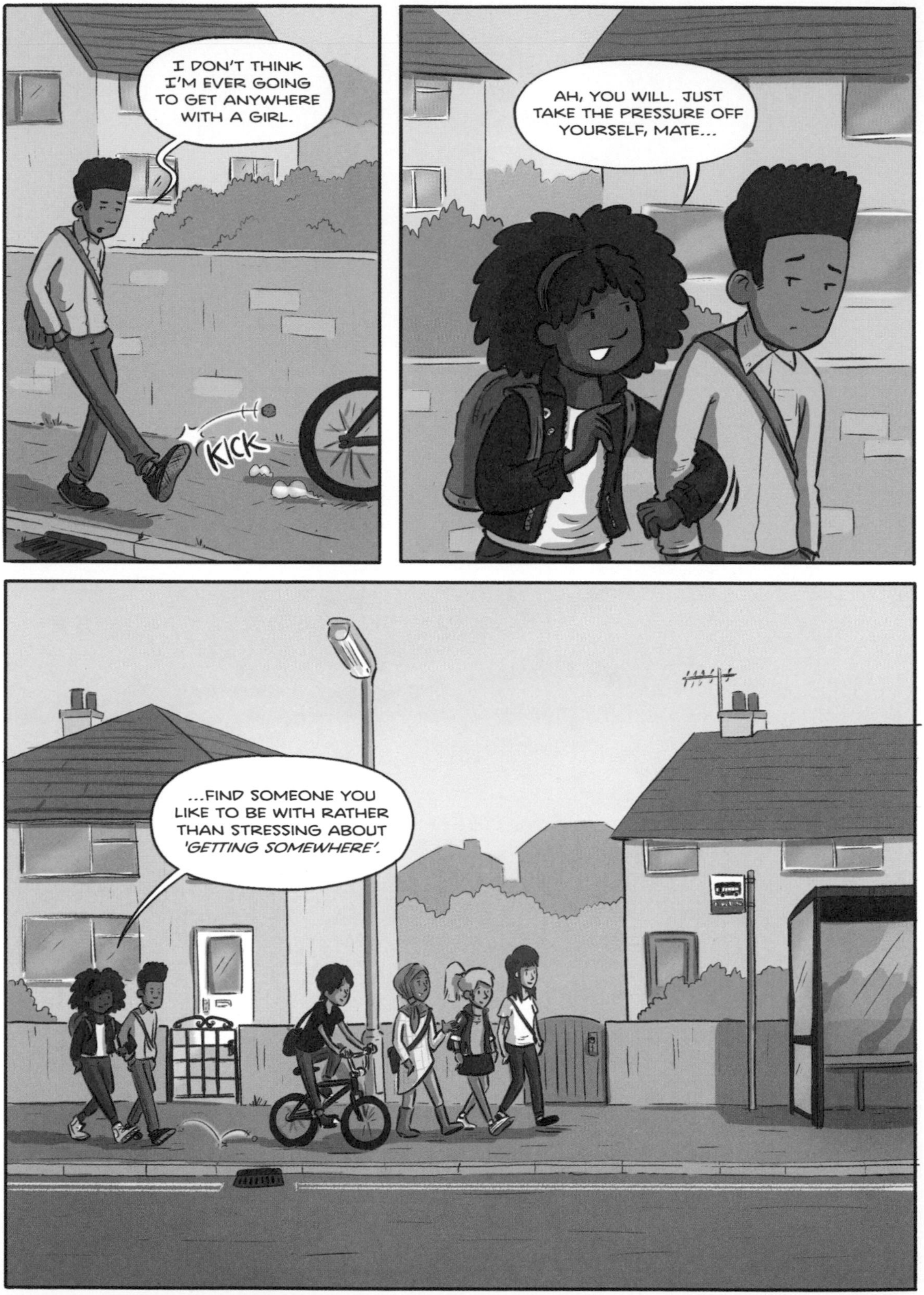
I DON'T THINK I'M EVER GOING TO GET ANYWHERE WITH A GIRL.
KICK
AH, YOU WILL. JUST TAKE THE PRESSURE OFF YOURSELF, MATE...
...FIND SOMEONE YOU LIKE TO BE WITH RATHER THAN STRESSING ABOUT *'GETTING SOMEWHERE'*.

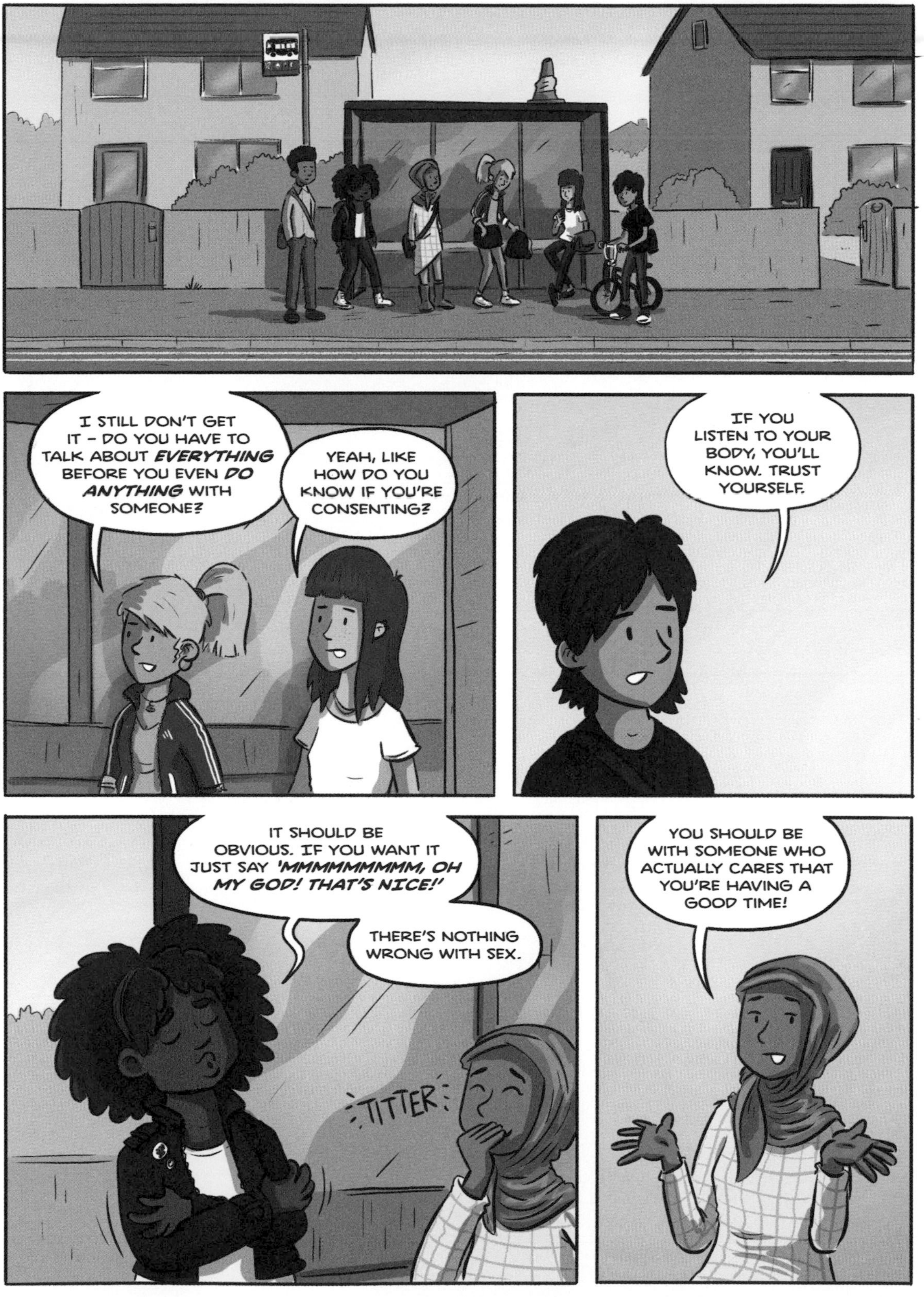
I STILL DON'T GET IT - DO YOU HAVE TO TALK ABOUT ***EVERYTHING*** BEFORE YOU EVEN ***DO ANYTHING*** WITH SOMEONE?
YEAH, LIKE HOW DO YOU KNOW IF YOU'RE CONSENTING?
IF YOU LISTEN TO YOUR BODY, YOU'LL KNOW. TRUST YOURSELF.
IT SHOULD BE OBVIOUS. IF YOU WANT IT JUST SAY ***'MMMMMMMMM, OH MY GOD! THAT'S NICE!'***
THERE'S NOTHING WRONG WITH SEX.
TITTER
YOU SHOULD BE WITH SOMEONE WHO ACTUALLY CARES THAT YOU'RE HAVING A GOOD TIME!

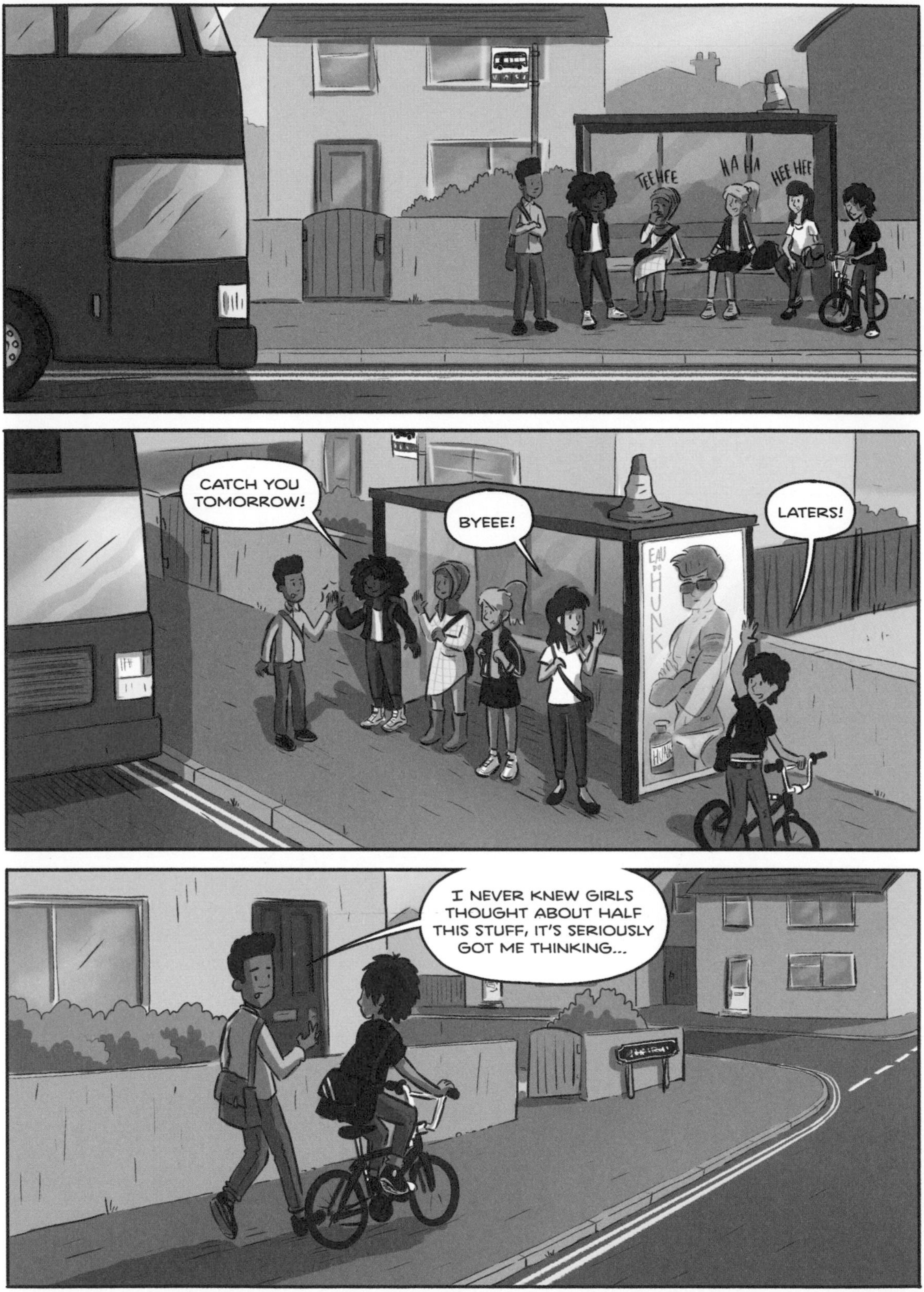
TEEHEE
HA HA
HEE HEE
CATCH YOU TOMORROW!
BYEEE!
EAU DO HUNK
LATERS!
I NEVER KNEW GIRLS THOUGHT ABOUT HALF THIS STUFF, IT'S SERIOUSLY GOT ME THINKING...

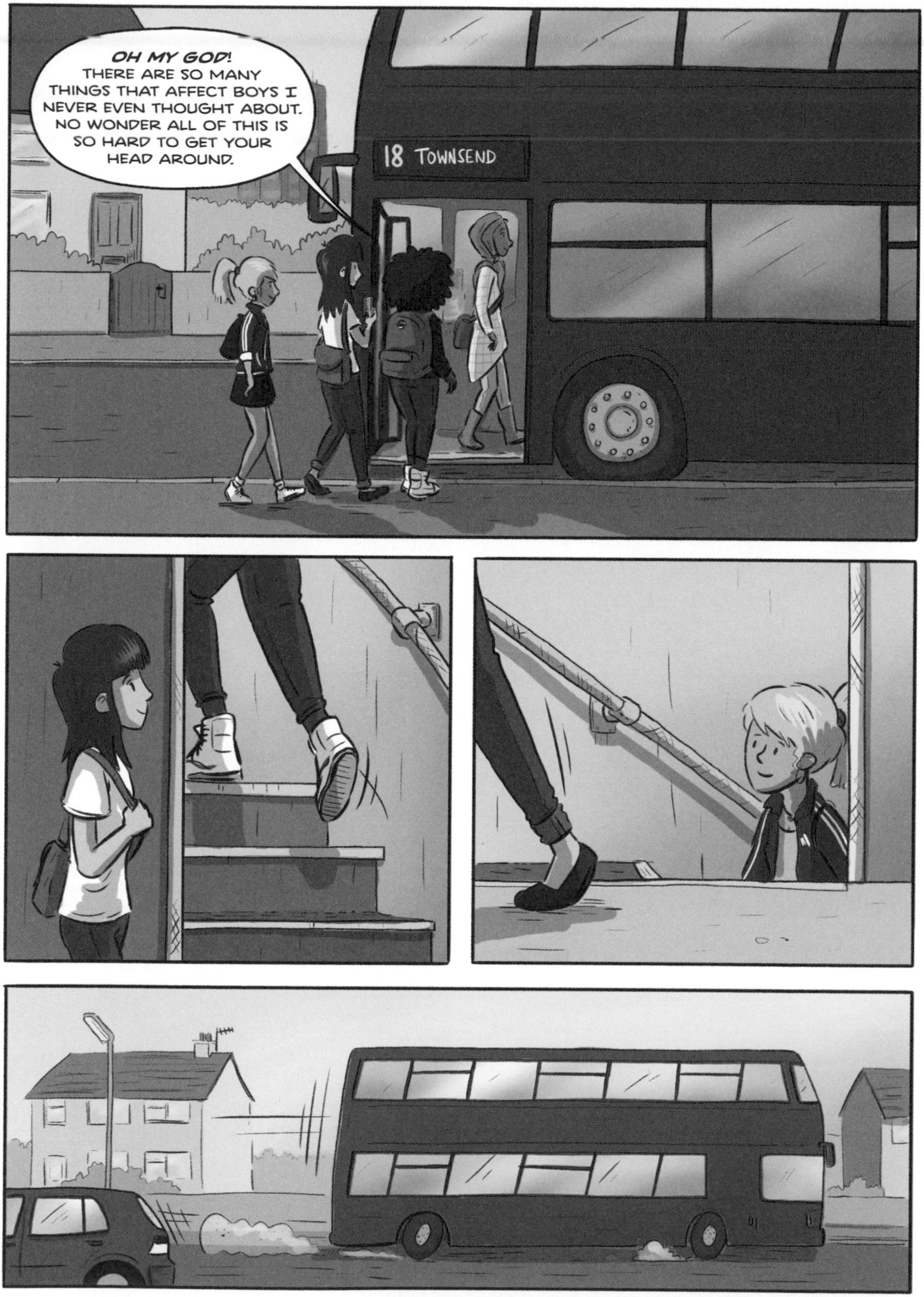
OH MY GOD! THERE ARE SO MANY THINGS THAT AFFECT BOYS I NEVER EVEN THOUGHT ABOUT. NO WONDER ALL OF THIS IS SO HARD TO GET YOUR HEAD AROUND.
18 TOWNSEND

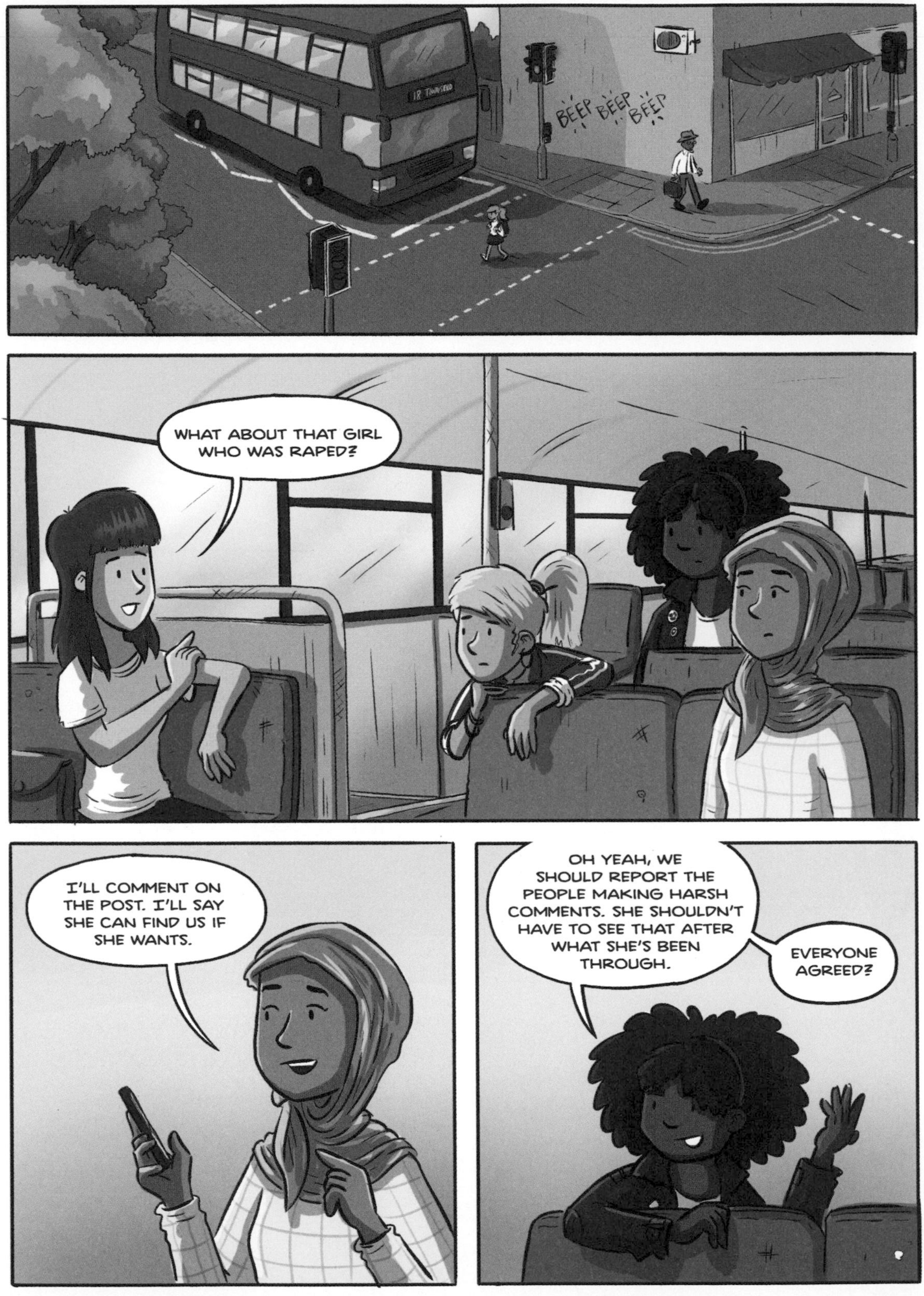
BEEP BEEP BEEP
18 TOWNSEND
WHAT ABOUT THAT GIRL WHO WAS RAPED?
I'LL COMMENT ON THE POST. I'LL SAY SHE CAN FIND US IF SHE WANTS.
OH YEAH, WE SHOULD REPORT THE PEOPLE MAKING HARSH COMMENTS. SHE SHOULDN'T HAVE TO SEE THAT AFTER WHAT SHE'S BEEN THROUGH.
EVERYONE AGREED?

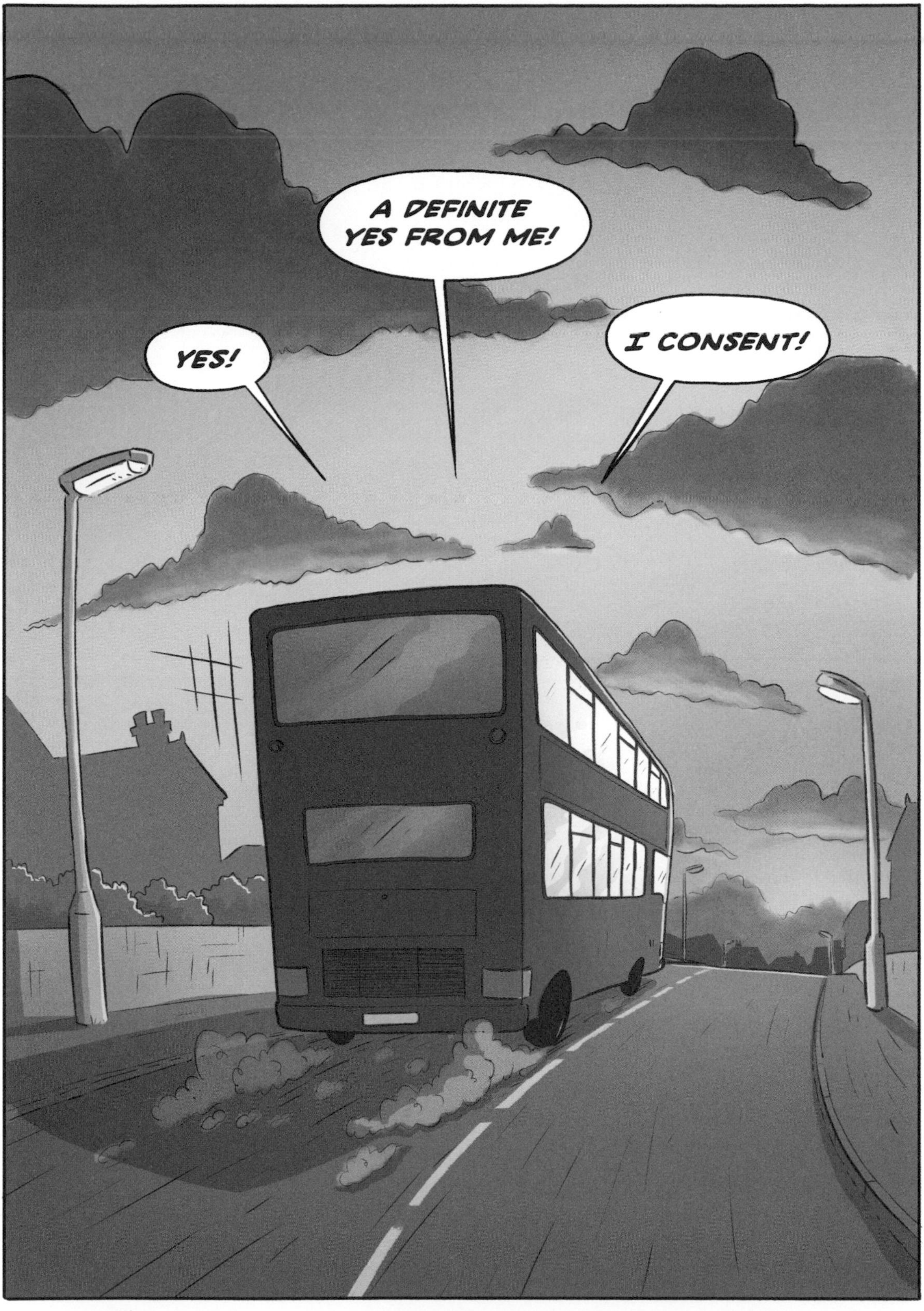
A DEFINITE YES FROM ME!
YES!
I CONSENT!

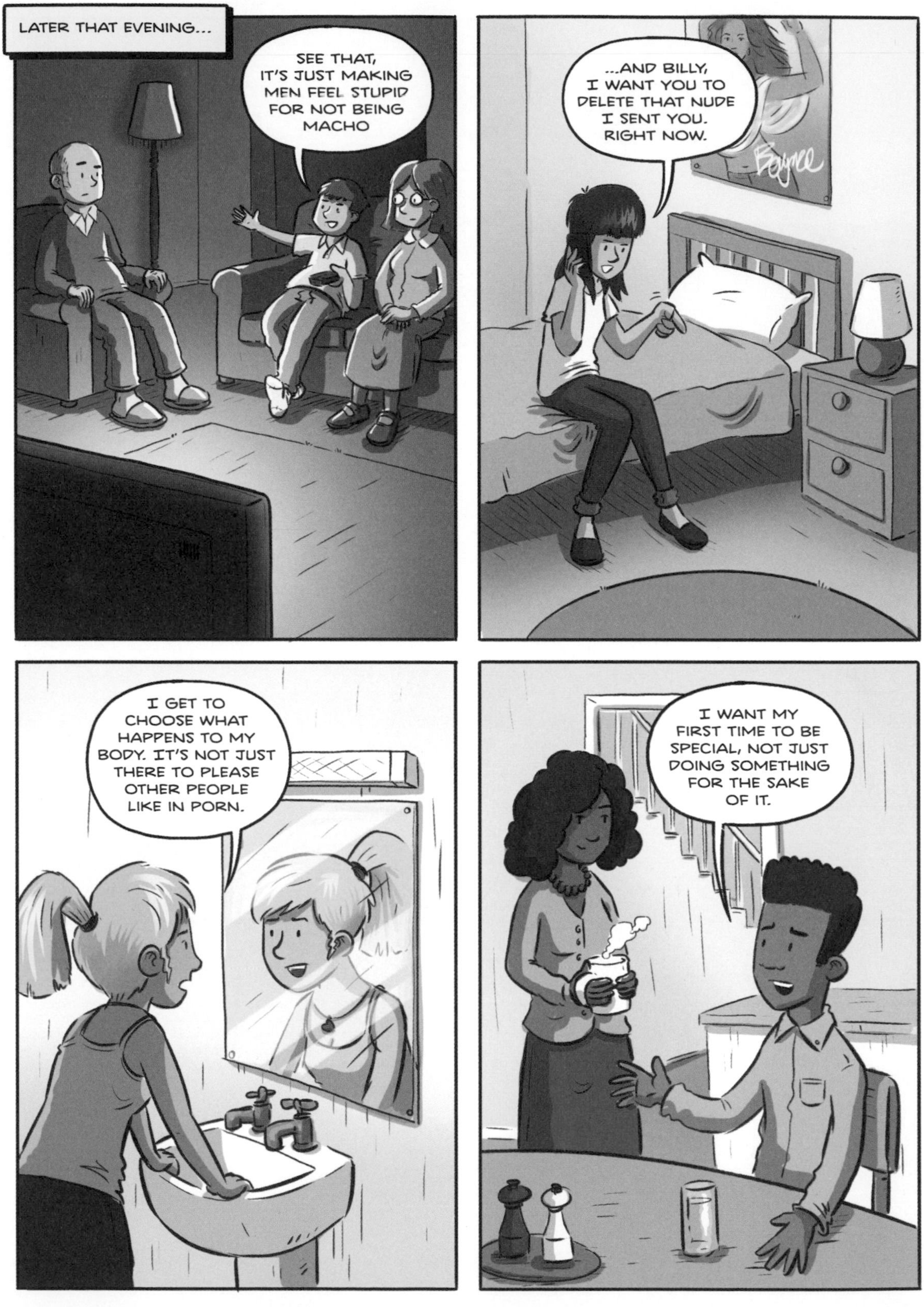
LATER THAT EVENING...
SEE THAT, IT'S JUST MAKING MEN FEEL STUPID FOR NOT BEING MACHO
...AND BILLY, I WANT YOU TO DELETE THAT NUDE I SENT YOU. RIGHT NOW.
I GET TO CHOOSE WHAT HAPPENS TO MY BODY. IT'S NOT JUST THERE TO PLEASE OTHER PEOPLE LIKE IN PORN.
I WANT MY FIRST TIME TO BE SPECIAL, NOT JUST DOING SOMETHING FOR THE SAKE OF IT.

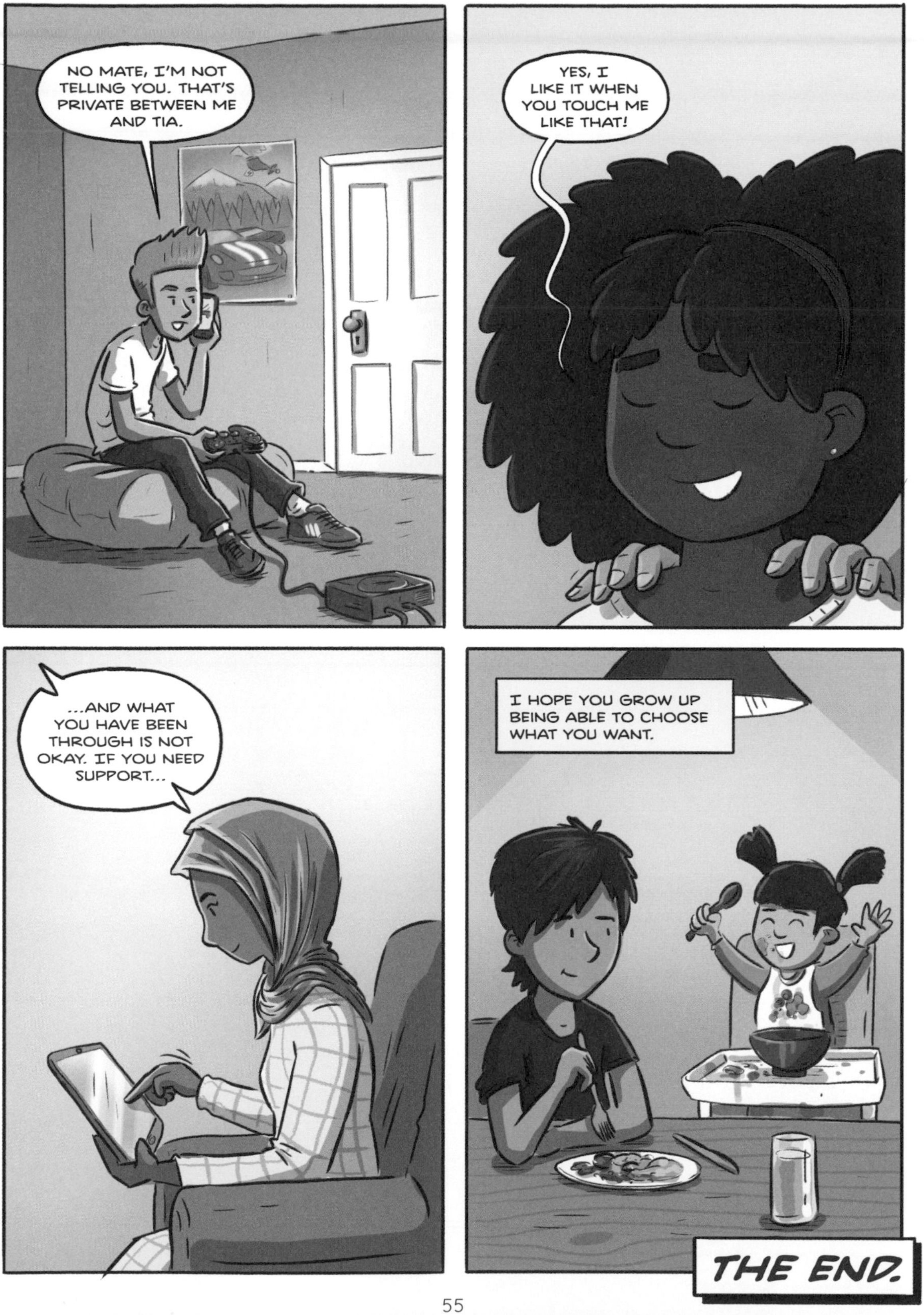
NO MATE, I'M NOT TELLING YOU. THAT'S PRIVATE BETWEEN ME AND TIA.
YES, I LIKE IT WHEN YOU TOUCH ME LIKE THAT!
...AND WHAT YOU HAVE BEEN THROUGH IS NOT OKAY. IF YOU NEED SUPPORT...
I HOPE YOU GROW UP BEING ABLE TO CHOOSE WHAT YOU WANT.
THE END.

What About You?

This section has some questions and information to get you thinking. There's loads of good stuff out there about sexual consent and the other issues raised in this cartoon. You will find some links to videos to watch and websites to browse.

If you are a parent, teacher, youth worker, mentor – or, in fact, any adult reading this – you can use *What Does Consent Really Mean?* as a resource to start a conversation with a young person, or to form the basis for a lesson or workshop on sex, healthy relationships and consent.

CONSENT

Discussion
1. How would you describe consent?
2. Why is consent important?
3. What are some of the signs that someone is pressuring you into sexual activity?

Did you know...?
- It is never okay to make or scare someone into doing something they don't want to.
- It's always okay to change your mind – it's your body and what you choose to do with it should be a free choice.
- Just because someone isn't saying NO it doesn't mean they are saying YES.

You could watch...
- *https://www.youtube.com/watch?v=fGoWLWS4-kU*: Cup of tea video

You could browse...
- *http://thatsnotcool.com*: Interactive scenarios, quizzes, cards and stats on friends and relationships
- *www.pauseplaystop.org.uk*: Equips young people to understand consent
- *www.thisdoesntmeanyes.com/#thisdoesntmeanyes*: Looks at myths and facts around consent
- *http://www.themix.org.uk/sex-and-relationships/single-life-and-dating/sexual-consent-15356.html*: Essential support for under-25s
- *http://thisisabuse.direct.gov.uk*: Support for young people in recognising and managing abuse
- *https://www.schoolsconsentproject.com*: Workshops and advice for schools with the aim of normalising conversations around consent and empowering young people

PORN

Discussion
1. Do you think porn is a good way to learn about sex and relationships?
2. If yes, how come, if no, why not?
3. Does porn reinforce traditional gender stereotypes?

Did you know...?
- Over 88% of the most popular porn scenes show acts of aggression.
- On average boys are exposed to porn age 10.
- It is illegal to watch or buy porn if you're under 18.
- More people access porn than YouTube and Netflix.

You could watch...
- *https://www.youtube.com/watch?v=g_HMSRA_-OE*: Creepy Online Stuff's video resource on porn

You could browse...
- *www.childline.org.uk/explore/onlinesafety/ pages/fapz-fight-against-porn-zombies.aspx*: Fight Against Porn Zombies – a resource for young people about pornography
- *https://www.nspcc.org.uk/services-and- resources/research-and-resources/2016/i- wasnt-sure-it-was-normal-to-watch-it*: NSPCC research into the impact of pornography on values, attitudes and behaviour
- *http://fightthenewdrug.org*: A campaign to raise awareness of the harmful effects of pornography

SEXTING AND NUDES

Discussion

1. Why do you think people might send someone a nude photo?
2. What are the risks of sending a nude photo or a sext?
3. People often do things online that they wouldn't do in real life – why do you think this is?
4. How can you be a good friend online?

Did you know...?

- To protect young people, it is illegal to have or to share indecent images of anyone under 18 (this is even true if the image is of yourself).
- You lose control over an image once you've pressed send.
- Revenge porn is now illegal.

You could watch...

- *www.safestories.org*: Four stories created by young people about online issues

You could browse...

- *www.thinkuknow.co.uk* (developed by CEOP): Resources exploring the risks children and young people face online, including three films that address the sharing of sexual images – 'Exposed', 'First to a Million' and 'Selfies: the naked truth'
- *https://www.nspcc.org.uk/preventing-abuse/ keeping-children-safe/sexting*: Resources produced by the NSPCC to make it easier for children and young people to get help about 'sexting'
- *www.childline.org.uk/explore/onlinesafety/ pages/sexting.aspx*: Information for young people on sexting, pressure, reporting and protecting your digital footprint
- *http://swgfl.org.uk/products-services/online- safety/resources/So-You-Got-Naked-Online*: SWGFL is a charity providing education resources, including this one on sexting

POSITIVE SEX

Discussion
1. Why are relationships important?
2. What does a healthy relationship look like?
3. If you felt ready to have sex, how would you know and how would you communicate this to a partner?

Did you know...?
- Sex is meant to be pleasurable for everyone involved.
- Some young people identify as gender fluid or transgender, and may feel more boy on some days, more girl on other days, neither boy nor girl or something outside those categories.
- Around half of young people identify as heterosexual.

You could watch...
- *www.truetube.co.uk/film/screwball*: A video on having sex for the first time

You could browse...
- *http://brook.org.uk*: Health, relationships and well-being website (includes information on gender and abuse)
- *http://lovesmart.themix.org.uk*: Advice to tackle issues in relationships healthily (jealousy, self-confidence, communication)
- *www.mermaidsuk.org.uk*: Mermaids UK – support for individuals and families who feel at odds with their birth gender
- *http://genderedintelligence.co.uk*: Support for young trans people
- *www.sexandu.ca*: An informative website for sex education
- *www.bgiok.org.uk*: Information and advice for gay, lesbian, bisexual and unsure young people

MEDIA

Discussion

1. Does the media portray healthy relationships? Can you think of any examples (soap operas, song lyrics, etc.)?
2. What is a stereotypical girl? What is a stereotypical boy?
3. What pressures do stereotypes put on young people?
4. What happens if we don't fit into the stereotypes? Is this fair?
5. What could we do as a group to move away from the pressure to fit in?

Did you know...?

- The media can influence our body image.
- The media can make things that are risky, dangerous or unhealthy seem normal.
- Most photos of people that we see in the media are Photoshopped.

You could watch...

- *https://vimeo.com/114048986*: A video about the onslaught of media expectations on girls
- *https://www.youtube.com/watch?v=-_l17cK1ltY*: Shows how media images of men are created using Photoshop

You could browse...

- *www.Mediasmart.uk.com*: Media Smart have developed a set of teacher's notes and a lesson plan on body image, which introduces the connection between the media and young people's perceptions of body image
- *http://raisingchildren.net.au*: Some interesting ideas on media and its influences
- *www.net-aware.org.uk*: Advice for practitioners and parents to understand social media

RESILIENCE

Discussion

1. What physical sensations do you notice in your body when you are feeling unsafe or uncomfortable?
2. Who would you be comfortable talking to if you were worried?
3. How could you be a good friend if someone turned to you?
4. What can we do to keep our minds and our bodies healthy?
5. What is an example of positive risk-taking?

Did you know...?

- When our body is in danger – or thinks it is – it can respond automatically by Fighting, Flighting (running away), Freezing, Flopping/Fainting or by trying to make Friends with whatever it is that's making us scared. Our body does this to try to protect us and keep us safe.
- Working out who we are can be difficult. Our brains don't develop fully until well into our twenties!

You could watch...

- *https://www.youtube.com/watch?v=hiduiTq1ei8*: Explains how the teenage brain works

You could browse...

- *www.childline.org.uk* and *www.ceop.police. uk/safety-centre*: If you are concerned about anything to do with the topics discussed above, you can refer to Childline or the CEOP website
- *https://youngminds.org.uk*: Lots of information for young people on wellbeing and mental health
- *http://mindfulnessforteens.com*: Mindfulness awareness practices for teenagers
- *www.howtothrive.org*: An organisation providing resilience training for schools